TOO LATE TO DIE

Too Late to Die

Bill Crider

Walker and Company
New York

Copyright © 1986 by Bill Crider

First published in the United States of America in 1986 by the Walker Publishing Company, Inc.

Published simultaneously in Canada by John Wiley & Sons Canada, Limited, Rexdale, Ontario.

Library of Congress Cataloging-in-Publication Data

Crider, Bill, 1941-
  Too late to die.

  I. Title.
PS3553.R497T6   1986   813'.54   85-31481
ISBN 0-8027-5650-6

Printed in the United States of America

10 9 8 7 6 5 4 3 2 1

FOR MY PARENTS
AND OF COURSE FOR JUDY, ANGELA,
AND ALLEN

1

IT WAS ANOTHER damn election year, and if there was one thing that Sheriff Dan Rhodes knew for sure it was that Hod Barrett wasn't going to vote for him this time either.

Unfortunately, that didn't mean that Barrett could just be ignored. As sheriff of Blacklin County, Texas, Rhodes was obliged to listen to Barrett's complaints and even try to help him out when his little grocery store got robbed, which seemed to be about every two or three weeks here lately.

"It's just some damn kids, Sheriff Rhodes," Barrett said, jamming his big, blocky fists deep down in his pockets. He was about as tall as an anvil sitting on an oak stump, and just as solid. Thin, bristly red hair stuck straight up all over his head, and his face was almost as red as his hair. "They don't never take nothing but a few cartons of smokes and some beers. Maybe a Moon Pie or two. Looks like you could catch a bunch of damn kids, or at least give us folks here in Thurston a reg'lar patrol."

Thurston, according to the green and white City Limit sign not a quarter of a mile from Barrett's store, had a population of 408. It was seven miles from Clearview, the county seat. Rhodes considered these facts for a second or two. "Well, Hod," Rhodes said, "if you could persuade the commissioners to hire me five or six more deputies, I'm sure we could have one of them spend lots of time around here. As it stands right now, though, the best I can do is send one through every now and then. Johnny Sherman was by here last night, if he followed his route."

Hod shoved his hands even further down in his jeans, not

quite hard enough to cause the brass rivets to pop off the stitching at the top. "That Johnny Sherman couldn't find his butt with both hands," he said.

"Now, Hod," Rhodes said patiently, "you know that's not so, but if you don't like the way we're doing things over at the county seat, maybe you and some of the folks here in Thurston could get together and hire yourselves a town marshal."

Hod made a face and looked like he was about to strangle. "It's the sheriff's responsibility to protect us and our property!" he said in a choked voice. "We pay your salary with our taxes. You're elected by the people of this county, and you're supposed to protect us from damn thieving kids!"

The two men were standing on the cracked gray sidewalk in front of Hod's store, shaded by a heavy wooden awning. Rhodes looked through the screen doors of the store with their faded Rainbow Bread stencils. He could see some of the old men on the red loafer's bench by the soft drink cooler lean forward and perk up their ears. One of them spit a stream of snuff into a styrofoam cup he held in his left hand. Any minute now, they would get up the nerve to walk outside and join in the conversation. Rhodes didn't want to make a campaign speech, so he changed the subject.

"Tell you what, Hod," he said. "Let's us go take a look at where the break-in was."

The appearance of positive action calmed Barrett slightly, and he led the sheriff around to the back of the store. The grass in the alleyway was mowed short; even that around the building was trimmed. Barrett often boasted to his friends that he bought his wife the best lawn mower available.

On the ground by the red brick wall of the store lay an old evaporative cooler that had been set up on a wooden stand. The remains of the stand were scattered around. Whoever had broken into the store had simply knocked, or kicked, the stand from under the cooler, which had then fallen to the ground, pulled by its own weight. That had left a rectangular

2

hole in the wall about three feet up, easy enough to crawl through even if you were just a kid.

"Last time they broke out my restroom window and then kicked the door to the storeroom open," Barrett said, disgusted.

"Maybe somebody just finds this place too easy to break into," Rhodes suggested mildly.

"Now just a damn minute, Sheriff," Barrett protested, bringing his hands out of his pockets for the first time and waving them in the air like catchers' mitts. "You got no call . . ."

Whatever he had been about to say was interrupted by the sound of a car humming up the gravel road that ran beside the store. They turned to look just as the driver threw on his brakes and brought the automobile to a sliding, fishtailing stop. White dust settled over them, pushed by the car's momentum and a slight westerly breeze. Then Bill Tomkins catapulted himself out of the driver's seat, yelling, "Sheriff Rhodes, Sheriff Rhodes, you gotta come quick! Elmer Clinton's done killed his wife!"

Two minutes later Rhodes pulled up in Elmer Clinton's yard, scattering about thirty bantam hens and one scrawny rooster in all directions. The white frame house looked peaceful enough, shaded by a couple of big chinaberry trees, but the front door was standing open behind the screen. Rhodes got out of his car and started up on the porch. He had his right foot on the second of the two cement steps when Bill Tomkins and a load of the loafers from Barrett's store drove up.

"Don't anyone get out of that car," Rhodes yelled as he stepped up on the porch. "I'll put every damn one of you in jail."

Bill Tomkins turned off his engine, but nobody in the car moved. Rhodes opened the screen and went on in the house.

It was cool and dim inside, but not so dim that Rhodes had

3

any trouble spotting Jeanne Clinton. She was lying in the small living room about seven or eight feet from the front door. The room looked as if a storm had blown through it. A platform rocker, its cushions printed with early American designs, was overturned, and a heavy glass lamp had been shattered against the wall. An end table lay on its side, and magazines were scattered around the room. A *Redbook* and a *Cosmopolitan* lay by the end table. Beside Jeanne Clinton's body there was a copy of *TV Guide* with J. R. Ewing smiling evilly from its cover. The throw rugs that had covered the hardwood floor were wadded together as if someone had skidded on them.

Rhodes walked over to the body, touching nothing. There was some blood, but not much. Jeanne Clinton's face had been pretty, but now it was bruised and cut. Her slim neck was twisted at an odd angle; Rhodes was no doctor, but he thought it was probably broken. Though there had obviously been quite a struggle, there seemed to be no other marks on the body. Jeanne had been wearing shorts and a halter, showing off her spectacular figure, and her smooth arms and legs were unmarked except for some slight discolorations on the upper left arm, where someone might have squeezed it tightly.

Rhodes looked around the rest of the house but saw nothing else that was disturbed—no open drawers or signs of robbery. He went back outside to deal with the crowd of curiosity seekers.

Bill Tomkins and his friends had gotten up enough nerve to get out of the car, but they hadn't moved away from it. They were leaning against its side, and Bill was telling them about finding the body.

Rhodes figured that as long as Bill was telling the story, he might as well tell it officially. "Come on up here on the porch, Bill," Rhodes called.

Tomkins, a storklike man with weathered skin and a prominent Adam's apple, reluctantly separated himself from his cronies and shuffled over to the house. He and Rhodes settled themselves on the edge of the porch.

"How'd you come to find her, Bill?" Rhodes asked.

Tomkins gestured toward the dirt road that ran in front of the house. "I live just up the road," he said. His voice had a slight wheeze in it, because Bill smoked a lot. "Nearly every day I have to go get something or other at Hod's store, like biscuits or milk maybe, and when I passed by here today I saw that the front door was open. So I just thought I'd stop by, you know, like a neighbor, and say hello to Elmer. That's when I found her." His voice trailed off.

"Bill," Rhodes said quietly, "Elmer's car's gone. You can see the ruts right over there by that chinaberry tree where he parks it." The sheriff pointed over to their left where there were a couple of ruts and a patch of oil in the dirt between them. Two chickens were scratching in the ruts, and shriveled yellow berries with their stems still clinging to them lay in the oil. "You make it a habit to stop by and say hello to old Elmer when he's not at home, do you?"

The day was already warm, though it was still early, but Tomkins was sweating more than seemed natural. "No, Sheriff," he wheezed. "Course not, but, uh, . . . I, well, . . ."

Rhodes let him dangle for a second. Then he spoke. "You trying to tell me that Elmer might have had a reason to kill his wife? He's not here, but you said he did it, remember? Did you say that because you think he might've wanted to?"

Tomkins's head wobbled on his thin neck as he gave a negative shake. Then he appeared to change his mind. "Hell, I'll tell you. You'd find out quick enough anyways. Elmer works at the cable plant in Clearview, the twelve to eight shift. He usually don't get home till around nine-thirty or ten, eats breakfast at some cafe—supper to him I guess—'fore he comes home. Sometimes I stop by and talk to Jeanne on my way to the store. Just talk, that's all. She was a nice, friendly girl. But I ain't never been here 'cept in the broad daylight. Not like some other folks."

"What other folks you got in mind, Bill?" Rhodes asked.

"I wasn't thinkin' of anyone in particular." Tomkins looked out at the men standing by his car. They hadn't moved, and they were watching the two men on the porch like a hawk watches a rabbit.

"You might as well tell me, Bill. This is a murder case we have here, and I know you wouldn't want to stand in the way of justice being done. Besides, like you say, I'll find out soon enough anyhow."

"I don't like to talk about my neighbors," Tomkins said, though not as reluctantly as he might have if he really meant it. "But there's Hod Barrett for one."

Rhodes thought about that for a while. Then he sent Tomkins and his friends on their way. As sheriff of Blacklin County, he had to perform the on-scene investigation.

Rhodes got his evidence kit and his old Polaroid camera out of the trunk of the county car. County funds did not suffice to make him a well-equipped investigator, but he knew what to do with what he had: photographs of the body; fingernail scapings; fingerprints, if any; all the little details. He wouldn't vacuum the room or the body like they would in some big-city police department, but he would be careful.

Rhodes didn't mind taking the time, but he wasn't convinced that anything he found would be of help. He was a man who believed in his instincts. He liked to talk to people, listen to their stories, size them up. If they had anything to hide, he could usually find it out. But physical evidence didn't hurt anything when it was available.

He found nothing significant. Oddly, there was not even anything under Jeanne's fingernails, as if she hadn't fought back, hadn't even scratched her assailant.

Rhodes thought about that for a while, too. Then he went into the kitchen to the telephone and called the justice of the peace and an ambulance.

*   *   *

After Jeanne Clinton was pronounced dead at the scene, her body was taken away in the ambulance. It would go to Dallas for the autopsy, and Rhodes knew that it would be several days before he got the results. Rhodes was in no particular hurry. It seemed pretty certain that Jeanne hadn't been raped, since the clothes were still on the body, and it appeared equally sure that she had died of a broken neck. Finding out who did it was all that mattered now, and to find that out he would have to find out who would have a reason to want her dead, either that or who would be mad enough to kill her in a quick and violent fit of temper and rage. Or maybe there was more to it than that. Not exactly the kind of case Rhodes needed in a reelection year.

Elmer Clinton still hadn't arrived home. Rhodes left Joe Tufts, the JP, there to give Clinton the news. Tufts and Clinton had gone to high school together. Rhodes started back to Clearview by way of one of the county roads. It was still early in the day, and the sheriff wanted to do some thinking before he talked to Hod Barrett again.

Rhodes had just crossed the plank bridge over Sand Creek when he spotted something lying in the bar ditch in a patch of tall Johnson grass. He pulled the car as far off the narrow road as he could and got out to take a look at what at first glance appeared to be a pile of discarded clothing. When he slammed the car door, the pile jumped up and started running.

It was Billy Joe Byron. On an ordinary day, Billy Joe would never have run from the sheriff, and Rhodes wouldn't have chased him, but this wasn't an ordinary day.

"Dammit, Billy Joe," Rhodes yelled, "Slow down. If I get a cut on me from this Johnson grass, I'm going to kick your butt."

Billy Joe paid no attention to Rhodes's threat. If Rhodes's quarry hadn't hung his pants leg trying to climb over a barbed-wire fence by the ditch, the sheriff might never have caught him. When Rhodes put his hand on Billy Joe's shoulder, Billy Joe fell backwards into the weeds and grassburrs,

7

tearing his pants leg from the knee to the cuff. He lay in the grass going "Uhh-uhh-uhh-uhh." There was dried blood on the front of his clothes.

Billy Joe Byron was a well-known character in Blacklin County. He wandered up and down all the roads and highways picking up aluminum cans to sell for twenty cents a pound, or whatever the current rate was. Before that, he'd picked up returnable bottles. He'd been making a living like that ever since Rhodes could remember. He had no other means of support. Most folks in Blacklin County figured that Billy Joe wasn't quite right in the head.

They were probably correct. A couple of years earlier, Rhodes had run him in a few times on Peeping-Tom charges, but other than that he'd never been in any trouble. He couldn't read or write, seldom talked, and seemed generally harmless. He stayed out of people's ways. Now here he was with dried blood on his clothes.

Rhodes sat down beside him on a spot relatively free of grassburrs. Billy Joe tried to burrow in the ground like an armadillo digging a hole, still going "Uhh-uhh-uhh-uhh." He'd never seemed afraid of Rhodes before, not even when he'd been arrested.

"Come on, Billy Joe," Rhodes said. "You know me. Sheriff Rhodes. You're not scared of me, are you?"

Billy Joe turned his head from the ground and looked up at the sheriff with little black eyes under bushy black brows. Something like recognition appeared in his glance. "N-n-not s-s-scared of y-you," he managed to get out. His face was as smooth and unlined as a child's, except for a few wrinkles around the eyes. There was dirt in the wrinkles.

"Good," Rhodes said. "How'd you like to take a little ride in the county car?" When he'd been arrested before, Billy Joe had always liked to ride in the car and had always wanted to turn on the lights and the siren. But not this time. He threw a look at the car, jumped up, and started running again.

Rhodes was caught off guard, but he got up and ran with

8

grim determination. He'd be damned if he was going to let Billy Joe escape from him. He'd never lost a prisoner.

This time Billy Joe didn't try to cross the fence, proving that he could learn from experience. He ran straight down the ditch, thrashing through Johnson grass that was sometimes over six feet tall. When he slowed to get his bearings, Rhodes caught up with him and threw his arms around his waist. Billy Joe writhed and turned as Rhodes struggled back to the car with him, but Rhodes held on. It was a little like trying to hold on to the Tasmanian Devil from the old Bugs Bunny cartoons, Rhodes thought, but he managed to do it. When they got back to the car, Rhodes held Billy Joe by the waistband of his pants, opened the back door, and shoved him in.

When Rhodes got in the driver's seat, Billy Joe was still squirming around in the back like a worm on a griddle. "Billy Joe," Rhodes said patiently, "this car is county property, and if you damage it you're going to be in big trouble. Now hold still." Billy Joe quieted down some, and Rhodes started the car.

In the confined space, Rhodes could smell Billy Joe, who had what could only be described as a distinctive odor. It was very likely, Rhodes thought, that Billy Joe had not had a bath since the last time he'd been in jail, two years before. Certainly, his clothes had never been washed. Rhodes detected a faint odor of beer along with the general ripeness that filled the car.

"When you're settled down a little, have a smoke," Rhodes said, pulling the car onto the road and turning on the air conditioner. He watched in the mirror as from somewhere in his filthy khaki shirt Billy Joe produced a soft pack of Merit Menthol 100s and a Bic lighter. Without offering a smoke to Rhodes, who didn't smoke anyway, Billy Joe lit up.

The Blacklin County jail might not have been a disgrace, exactly, but it wasn't the first place that anyone would want to point out to a visitor, either. It had been built in the early part of the century, when prisoners weren't too well thought of, and it had gotten considerably less comfortable over the years. It looked like a fortress from the dark ages, except that its exterior was brown sandstone, and instead of a moat it was surrounded by a stubby wrought-iron fence. The fence wouldn't keep anybody in or out, but no one on the outside wanted in, and those on the inside were kept in place by other barriers, like the heavily barred windows of the cells. The cells weren't air-conditioned, and they weren't very well heated in the winter. The walls were cracked, and the metal bed frames had rust spots on them. The plumbing was unreliable. A federal judge had recently given the county commissioners two years to do something about the conditions, something like building a new jail.

None of that mattered a bit to Billy Joe Byron. He'd been to jail before, and it compared favorably to the little shotgun shack covered with tar paper and composition shingles where he lived. This time, though, he didn't appear too eager to go inside. But Rhodes got him in.

Old Hack Jensen was over by the radio. The county was always strapped for money and couldn't afford a real dispatcher, but ever since Hack had retired from his job at the local Gulf station he'd helped out for far below the minimum wage.

"Who you got there, Sheriff?" Hack asked as Rhodes and Billy Joe came through the door. Then he did an exaggerated double take. "I'll be damned if it ain't old Billy Joe Byron, one of my favorite customers. What you been up to this time, Billy Joe?"

Billy Joe appeared glad to see Hack, so Rhodes let him go, and he walked over to the old man quite calmly. "Looks like maybe you and Billy Joe had yourselves a little tussle, Sheriff," Hack said, glancing at Rhodes's soiled uniform and the blood on Billy Joe's shirt. "Is that your blood or Billy Joe's there?"

"I've sort of been wondering about that blood myself," Rhodes said. "I don't think it's mine or his. See if you can rustle up an old shirt for Billy Joe to wear while he's with us. We may have to send that one to Houston for some lab tests. Where's Lawton?"

Lawton was the jailer, almost as old as Jensen. He'd been working for the county for over forty years, but they couldn't retire him. He was the only certified jailer they had.

"He's upstairs in the block," Hack said, referring to the second floor of the jail where the cells were located. "Johnny brought in a couple of guys last night, says they got in a fight out to the Paragon Club. He had to break it up, and they gave him a pretty bad time. I don't know who looks worse, him or them.

"And that reminds me," Hack went on. "Miz Kinchloe called a while ago, mighty upset. Her husband just kicked out the windshield of that little S-10 pickup they bought last week. What really bothered her is that she was in the pickup when he did the kicking."

"They're at it again, huh?" said Rhodes.

"You ain't lying," Hack said. "I guess it's just about time, though. She hasn't taken a shot at him for three or four weeks now."

"I took the gun away from her after the last time," Rhodes said. "It's locked up in the property closet."

"Damn good thing, too. Want me to send someone over there?"

"Not right now. I may drive by later. If they didn't have each other to fight with, they'd start in on the neighbors."

While Rhodes was speaking, Lawton walked into the room through the stairwell doorway. He and Hack, when they stood together, looked a little like Abbott and Costello would have looked if they'd still been alive, Rhodes thought. Hack was tall, with slicked down hair and a thin moustache that still had a little brown in it. Lawton was short and stout, not really fat, but with a large round stomach that started just under his chest. He was nearly seventy, but he still had an almost unlined, innocent face.

"Those Kinchloes are a mess, ain't they," Lawton said as he walked into the room. "But they ain't got nothing on them boys upstairs."

"They giving you any trouble?" Rhodes asked.

"No more than I can handle," Lawton said. "Mostly, they're just loud. Claim they wasn't doing nothin' to speak of and that Johnny roughed them up with no reason. Goin' to sue us for po-lice brutality." He grinned at the thought, showing that he still had all his teeth, slightly stained by the Tube Rose snuff that he insisted on dipping. He'd been dipping for years before professional football players had made the habit semi-respectable by shilling for the tobacco companies on TV.

"I'll talk to them about it later," Rhodes said. "You put Billy Joe, there, up in number five for the time being. Be sure to take his belt and shoelaces. Leave him his smokes, but take his lighter. We'll be wanting his shirt later." Rhodes turned to Hack. "Get Johnny Sherman down here for me."

"I expect he's home asleep by now, Sheriff," Hack said.

"That doesn't matter," Rhodes said. "It's not about those two drunks up there. This is something I didn't call in because I didn't want every scanner in the county broadcasting it. Jeanne Clinton's been killed over in Thurston."

12

2

"JESUS," JOHNNY SHERMAN said when Rhodes gave him the news. "I went to high school with Jeanne." Johnny was twenty-eight years old, and he'd been a deputy for three years. Before that he'd done a little bit of everything, Rhodes thought, including a couple of years in the army and a few months of serving as a bouncer at some high-toned club in Dallas. He was big and good-looking, if a little fast with his fists. He'd been a good deputy, but there was something about him that bothered Rhodes, something that he couldn't quite put into words. Lately, he hadn't even bothered to try. Johnny had kept his nose clean, and for the last month and a half he'd been dating Rhodes's daughter.

"Did you notice anything out of the way when you drove through Thurston last night?" Rhodes asked. "Seems like they had a regular crime wave over there."

Johnny looked at Rhodes with his pale gray eyes. "You mean there's more?"

"Yeah, there's more. Somebody broke in Hod Barrett's store again."

"Damn. That must have happened after I went by. There was nothing wrong then. That town is as quiet as a school on Saturday."

"Not anymore, it's not," Rhodes said.

"Right. Claymore's going to love this," Johnny said, rubbing his chin thoughtfully.

Ralph Claymore was Rhodes's opponent in the May election, less than a month away. He was ten years younger and, Rhodes was convinced, much better-looking than the present sheriff. He had wavy black hair with no gray in it, and he could wear tight-fitting western shirts without revealing the slightest bulge in the area of his belly. He wore western hats like he was born in them, and boots, and big silver belt buckles. Rhodes didn't like boots because they hurt his toes. He didn't have any silver buckles, and he knew that in a western hat he looked like a cat turd under a collard leaf. And now he had a murder on his hands. He might not look like a sheriff, but he was damn sure going to have to act like one.

"Yeah," Rhodes said. "Claymore's going to love this, all right, but if we get it cleared up in time, I'll be a shoo-in."

"That's true," Johnny said. "We'd better get on it."

"It'll have to wait for a minute or two," Rhodes said. "First you'd better tell me about those two guys from the Paragon."

"Not much to tell, really. I drove by there on the way in, and they were scuffling in the parking lot. I tried to stop them, and they got a little rough."

Rhodes looked Sherman over. His knuckles were scabbed over, and his face had a few superficial cuts on it. He'd been walking pretty carefully when he came in. "What time was all this?"

"Toward the end of the shift. Must have been about six-thirty. Pretty near sunup."

"They must have been pretty feisty for so early in the morning. That Paragon is livelier than I thought it was. Anyway, their story is that you're the one that started things. They say they're going to sue. Claymore would like that almost as much as the murder."

"Bullshit, they're going to sue." Johnny's size 16 neck began to get red. "I didn't lay a hand on them until they jumped me."

"That might be true," Rhodes said, "but if they sue, the case will still be up in the air until well after the election."

"I could resign," Johnny said.

"Well, let's don't jump the gun. Maybe we ought to talk to them about what happened."

14

Johnny slapped his right fist into his left palm. "That sounds like a good idea," he said. He got out of his chair, wincing a little.

They walked up to the block. The two men were in number four, right next to Billy Joe, and when Rhodes and Sherman got there Billy Joe started jabbering and backing up in his cell. He was all the way in the corner looking for a hole.

"What's the matter with you, Billy Joe?" Rhodes asked him, but he couldn't answer, or wouldn't. Rhodes turned to the men in the other cell.

"Is this the man you fellas want to sue?" Rhodes asked, pointing a thumb at Johnny Sherman.

"Damn right," said one of the men. He was about Rhodes's height, five-nine or -ten, with very black hair shot through with gray streaks. He had a scraggly gray and black goatee, and he was wearing a red and white cap with an armadillo on it. "We're gonna sue him and the whole damn county."

His friend, smaller but very tough-looking, something like James Cagney in *White Heat*, echoed him. "We're gonna get you all, the whole rotten bunch. Our civil rights've been violated. You can't get away with beating up on honest ciitzens."

Rhodes looked at Johnny Sherman's cut face. "Looks like we weren't the only ones doing the beating. You two aren't marked up any worse than my deputy here."

"Hell," said the one with the cap. "We never laid a hand on him. We was just trying to get in our car and get home before our wives got to worrying too much about us, and this sonuvabitch jumped us. I'll probably have to get divorced now, by god, and that's his fault too!"

Rhodes put his hand on Johnny Sherman's arm; he could feel the younger man's muscles tense through the cloth. He hoped that Johnny wouldn't reach out and grab one of the men by his shirtfront and try to jerk him through the bars.

"It'll all come out in court, boys," Rhodes said. "Assaulting an officer is a pretty serious thing."

"Assaulting is what he did to us, not what we did to him," said the Cagney look-alike. "And we'll prove it, too!"

"Goddamn liars!" Johnny burst out. "Just give me a few minutes with 'em, Sheriff, and we'll see . . ."

Rhodes gently pressured Johnny's arm and pushed him back from the cell. "Don't worry about these two, Johnny," he said. "You go on home now and get some rest. We'll take care of this later. I've got to go back over to Thurston and talk to Elmer Clinton and Hod Barrett."

"Goddamn liars," Johnny muttered again as he and Rhodes walked back toward the stairs.

Billy Joe Byron huddled in the corner of his cell and whimpered.

Elmer Clinton was sitting in his living room drinking a Coors Light when Rhodes arrived. Rhodes had stopped for lunch at Sally's Truck Stop, but it appeared from the number of empty aluminum cans scattered around the room that Elmer was sticking to a liquid diet. He'd done nothing to clear up the mess, and there were still spots of blood on the floor. He didn't even get up when Rhodes tapped at the door facing. "Come on in, Sheriff," he said, taking another sip of his Coors.

Rhodes opened the screen and stepped in, giving Elmer a quick once-over. Clinton was a stout man, only about five-six or so, but heavy, with massive arms and legs. His dirty-blond hair was thinning on top, and his close-set eyes reminded Rhodes of Lloyd Bridges.

"How're you making it, Elmer?" Rhodes asked.

Clinton took a long pull at his beer can, tossed it aside, and popped open another. "I'm makin' it, Sheriff," he said, his words only slightly slurred. "That's about all. That's about all." He took a drink from the fresh can.

"I hate to have to ask you these things, Elmer," Rhodes said, "but it's what has to be done. You have any ideas about this? Know any reason why someone might want to kill

16

Jeanne? Any enemies? Any big fusses with anyone here in town?"

Elmer looked at the floor. "There was nothing, not a thing," he said. "Everyone loved Jeanne. Why, that girl wouldn't hurt a fly, much less cause trouble amongst the folks here in town." He shot a quick glance in Rhodes's direction. "I know you might've heard things about how she was a little wild, all that stuff that got out after she won that wet T-shirt contest at the Paragon that time, but that was a long time ago. She's not like that"—he shook his head angrily—"I mean, she *wasn't* like that anymore. She was just tryin' to be a good wife to me. Lord knows, I loved that girl, Sheriff."

Rhodes was sometimes uncomfortable in the presence of what he took to be sentimentality, especially sentimentality that had a suspiciously false note in it. This was one of those times, and he wondered just what Elmer was trying to hide. He'd come in determined to spare Elmer's feelings, but now he decided to give a jab or two in tender areas and see what happened.

"What time do you leave for work every night, Elmer?" Rhodes asked.

"Usually about fifteen or twenty till twelve," Clinton said. "It don't take very long to get there, and the roads are clear by that time of the night. No traffic at all."

"Was Jeanne in the habit of walking around the house in shorts and a halter at that time of night, even after you'd left?"

Clinton rolled the Coors can between his palms. "I don't know what you mean, Sheriff," he said. "It's pretty hot for April, if that's what you're getting at."

"That's not it exactly, Elmer," Rhodes said, looking at Clinton's face, trying to watch his eyes instead of the silver and black can that he was rolling slowly between his palms. "I mean that you'd already gone. I mean that maybe she was dressed up for somebody else."

Elmer crushed the thin metal can, and beer spewed up and

17

over his hands, spilling on the floor and running under the *Redbook* that lay nearby. "By damn, Sheriff! Don't you dare say a thing like that about my Jeanne! She wasn't seein' anybody! There wasn't nobody for her but me! Understand?"

Rhodes had gotten more of a reaction than he anticipated. "I understand, Elmer. I wasn't trying to imply something that would make Jeanne look bad. I just thought that if she had a regular visitor, you know, we might have a starting place."

Elmer slumped back in the platform rocker in which he sat and reached for another beer. "No visitors," he said. "No matter what anyone else tells you. No visitors."

Rhodes decided to drop the subject for the time being, but it was clearly something that he needed to check up on. He took a different approach. "OK, Elmer, if you say so, it must be true. No visitors. I'll just have to think about something else. By the way, why were you so late getting home this morning?"

"Wasn't so late. Don't usually get here until around ten or so. Have a little breakfast, talk to the boys. You know. I was at Sally's this morning."

That would be easy enough for Rhodes to check. He'd already called the cable plant, and Clinton had worked his full shift. He'd have Johnny Sherman or one of the other deputies check at Sally's to make sure Elmer had been there, too. "Well, that's about it for now, Elmer," he said. "I guess I'll have some more questions later; maybe one of the boys will be by instead of me. Don't go off anywhere so we can't find you, hear?"

"I hear, Sheriff, I hear. You just find out who killed Jeanne. Then you let me have a few minutes with him. That's all I'm asking."

As Rhodes walked back onto the porch, Clinton was staring off into space with unfocused eyes and swallowing beer.

Hod Barrett's little grocery store was caught in its usual mid-afternoon lull. There were no customers, except for two old men on the loafer's bench, and it wasn't likely that either of them was going to buy anything. Rhodes pulled open the left screen and walked in.

The store was much darker than most modern groceries. It was lit by three fly-specked hundred-watt bulbs that hung down from the ancient stamped-tin ceiling by twisted, fabric-covered cords. The floor was the same cement as the walk out front, stained darker from years of spills and sweepings. There were shelves along the walls to Rhodes's left and right, and a long two-sided shelf in the middle. To his left was the bench and the soft-drink cooler, a very old one in which the drinks sat up to their necks in icy water circulated by a small pump. To his right was the glass candy case, filled mostly with hard candy and gum. The store wasn't air-conditioned, and chocolate tended to melt.

Hod Barrett was at the back of the store beside the meat cooler that separated his small butcher shop from the rest of his stock. He was leaning over a counter working on his accounts. About the only way he could keep any customers was to offer credit; otherwise, everyone in town would drive to the Safeway in Clearview. Beside Barrett was an old cash register that doubled as his adding machine when he worked on the accounts.

"Figuring your taxes, Hod?" Rhodes joked as he strolled to the rear of the store.

"Already done that," Barrett replied. "Next time I ought to get a lot of money back, considering all my losses to thieves that you can't catch." He flipped an account book shut with a snap and stuffed it in a file.

"Does Elmer Clinton have an account in there, Hod?" Rhodes asked.

Barrett looked up. "Of course he does. Nearly everybody in town has an account with me, large or small. You can't drive all the way to Clearview when you need a quart of milk, and if you can get credit you take it."

"Is Elmer's account one of the large ones or one of the small ones?"

Barrett didn't even have to check his account books. "It's

19

one of the small ones. I think Elmer buys most of his groceries before he comes home after work. He has to drive over to Clearview anyway. I don't hold it against him. What's all that got to do with my store being robbed, anyway?"

Rhodes shrugged. "Nothing, probably. But your robbery kind of has to take second place now that Jeanne Clinton's been killed."

Barrett started to protest, but Rhodes went on without giving him an opening. "I guess it was Jeanne that did most of the buying here, and not Elmer."

Barrett nodded. "That's right. She came in every day or so for little items. Bread. Milk. Laundry powder. Never bought more than two or three items at a time. Always put them on the bill, always paid right on the first."

"How well did you get to know Jeanne, Hod?" Rhodes inquired mildly.

Barrett shoved his account file aside roughly and started around the counter. "Now, see here, Sheriff, I'll have you know . . ."

"Now, Hod, don't get your blood pressure all elevated," Rhodes said. "I just thought you might be able to tell me if she had any enemies here in town, anyone that might want to do away with her. I don't believe a single thing was stolen from that house, like there was from your store, and since you live right nearby I thought you might be able to give me a lead."

Barrett pushed both hands down on the counter and took a deep breath, visibly getting control of himself. "OK, Sheriff, I see what you mean. I just thought . . . never mind. No, I don't know of anyone who didn't like Jeanne. She was a nice friendly girl." A thought seemed to strike him. "Say, you don't think there could be any connection between the robbery here and the killing, do you?"

"Now that's a right interesting idea, Hod," Rhodes said. "Can't say as I've given it any real consideration, but now that you mention it, I'll give it some thought."

Barrett had a disgusted look on his face, which indicated his idea of the dim mental processes of the county's law enforcement officers. If he had to give them all their ideas, he seemed to be thinking, then things were really in a mess.

"By the way, Hod," Rhodes said, interrupting Barrett's thoughts, "Do you think your wife might be able to tell me any more than you have about Jeanne? I mean, seeing as how you all live so close by her and all. Not more than a block away, is it? Since Miz Barrett stays home most of the day, she might have seen something more than you."

Barrett's stocky body didn't move, but his Adam's apple rose and fell several times as if he were swallowing a golf ball. His voice, when he spoke, was thin and forced. "You stay away from my wife, Sheriff," he said. "She don't know nothing, and she won't have nothing to tell you."

"You seem a little tense today, Hod," Rhodes said kindly. "I know this robbery has you on edge, and you probably aren't thinking too straight. But you know that there's been a murder, and it's my job to ask questions of anybody that might have information. You understand that, don't you?"

Barrett's arms went limp and dangled at his sides. For the first time Rhodes noticed how long they were, way out of proportion on Barrett's chunky body, like the arms of an ape. He must be hell to buy shirts for, Rhodes thought.

"Yeah, I understand," Barrett said. "I just didn't think it was necessary."

"You never know, Hod," Rhodes said, turning and walking to the front of the store. "You just never know."

He glanced at the two old men as he passed by the loafer's bench. Their ears looked like they were growing on stalks. Rhodes smiled, stopped, and handed each one of them one of his cards.

3

DRIVING BACK TO Clearview, Rhodes thought about his conversations with Clinton and Barrett. Both men were obviously nervous, both on edge, but that didn't necessarily mean anything. Rhodes knew that anyone involved in the investigation of a serious crime was likely to feel nervous. Everyone seemed to feel guilty about something or other, even if it wasn't something directly or even indirectly related to the crime under investigation. He would trust his instincts and keep on probing, asking questions, talking to anyone involved in the case, and eventually he'd find out what he wanted to know. He was sure of that.

He thought about some of the questions he would have to ask as he drove the county car toward Clearview, oblivious of the bluebonnets that grew in state-planned profusion by the side of the road. He was not so wrapped up in his thoughts, however, that he missed the huge sign, done in red, white, and blue, that advertised Ralph Claymore's candidacy for sheriff. It was firmly affixed to a farmer's fence. If it had been on public property, Rhodes would have pulled it down.

When Rhodes got back to the jail, Hack was ready with all the news. "Those two guys that Johnny brought in have walked. Their wives got up their bail money."

"I figured on that," Rhodes said. "We probably don't have to worry too much about any lawsuit from those two. They're glad to be gone."

"Right. Buddy Reynolds brought in a couple a while ago, by the way."

22

Hack paused. He had a way of wanting Rhodes to draw things out of him.

"A couple of birds."

"Birds? What kind of birds?"

"Lovebirds," Hack said. "Tried to set up housekeepin' in the city park. Trouble was, all they had was a quilt. Charged 'em with adultery."

Rhodes laughed. "Buddy always has been a narrow-minded devil. What happened?"

"Well, it turns out they're married, but not to each other. So we called the husband and wife and the district judge. The judge told us to release the lovebirds into their spouses' custody and he'd have them make an appearance before him later."

"Where's Buddy now?"

"We got a call about a wreck over toward Milsby. Buddy's on the way over to help out the highway patrol. Don't think it's a bad one, though."

"Good," Rhodes said. The mention of Milsby had reminded him that he was supposed to appear at a candidates' forum and cake auction there that night. It wasn't something he was looking forward to, but he had to be there. Ralph Claymore sure would. "What about Billy Joe?"

"He seems to be doing OK. Ate a pretty good lunch. Just sits on the cot most of the time, humming to himself."

"Any word from the state boys on that shirt of his?"

"Hell, Sheriff, you know better than that. If we hear within a week, we'll be doing good."

"Good's not good enough in this case. Give them a call and tell them it's an emergency. Same with the autopsy on Jeanne Clinton."

Hack looked skeptical. "I'll give it a try," he said, "but I wouldn't count on it doin' any good."

"Try anyway," Rhodes told him. "I'm going over to the house to get ready for that forum tonight. Put any important calls through to me there, but save the routine stuff for Buddy or Bob. Where's Bob, by the way?"

"We got a call from some woman out by the rock crusher, says her kid found a pickup stripped and abandoned in the field out behind their house. Might be the one that was stole from Larry Harper night before last."

"Who's going to tow it in?"

"Five Star."

"OK. Tell you what. I want Buddy and Bob to take all the routine stuff. I'll probably be through at the cake auction before they go off shift, but tell them I'll be devoting all my time to the Clinton case if I don't see them."

Hack nodded. "Right, Sheriff, I'll do that for sure." As Rhodes was leaving, Hack started for the radio.

Clearview was a town of about eight thousand people, and like any town of that size it had clearly established neighborhoods. Some were new, and the houses in them were large and expensive. A few backyards even had swimming pools in them, and the lawns were kept green and trimmed by black or Chicano yardmen. The people living in these neighborhoods were generally fairly young, many of the men holding some sort of executive position at the cable company or the decorative products factory, both located in the optimistically named "industrial park" area of the town. So far these were the only two industries of any size located there, but the city council members had great hopes for the future.

There were large and impressive houses in other neighborhoods, too, but these were older homes, huge, two-story stone structures resembling, somewhat, small castles or lavish haciendas. They had been built in the 1920s and 1930s, when Clearview had experienced a minor oil boom. The boom hadn't lasted for very long, but it had proven quite profitable for some of the landowners at the time. Their descendants lived on in their old homes, quite comfortable, insulated for the most part from the daily life of the community by their money and their social position.

Quite the reverse was true in the area called "the flats."

Most of the black and brown population lived there in board shacks with hard-packed dirt yards. Their porch roofs sagged, and the yard furniture often consisted of an old automobile seat or a decrepit living-room couch cast off by one of the well-to-do families from the better neighborhoods. Small, ragged children could occasionally be seen sleeping outside on warm nights, sharing the buckled and sprung couch with a dog or a scrawny chicken.

Sheriff Dan Rhodes lived in none of these areas. He lived instead in an older part of the town that had once been quite respectable but which was now on the way down. Most of the yards were still neatly kept, and there were certainly more and larger trees than in the newer additions to the city's residential sections, but many of the frame houses needed paint. Some had needed it for quite a while. Some could also have used new roofs, while others displayed wire screens that were rusted with age.

The house where Rhodes lived was about average for the block on which it was located. White paint on the wooden sides peeled only slightly. The cement sidewalk that ran from the front door to the street was slightly buckled, but no grass grew in the cracks. The shrubs around the house were neatly trimmed. In the front yard, a huge pecan tree shaded the freshly cut lawn.

Very little of this appearance was due to Rhodes's own care. He hated yard work and would do almost anything to avoid it. But his daughter seemed to enjoy it, and he was glad she did. He didn't mind living in a well-kept home. In fact, he liked it, as long as he didn't have to do too much of the work.

He parked the county car in the driveway and walked to the front door. It was four o'clock, and Kathy would most likely be at home. Rhodes pushed open the front door and called her name.

"I'm in the kitchen, Dad," she answered.

Rhodes walked back through the living room and a short hall to the kitchen, where his daughter was putting groceries from a sack into a white metal cabinet that stood against the wall next to an equally white refrigerator. She was twenty-three years old, not quite two years away from her college days at the state university in Huntsville where she had taken her degree in elementary education. After graduation she had gotten a job in Clearview to be close to her terminally ill mother, and after Claire Rhodes's death eighteen months ago Kathy had remained at home to look after her father.

Rhodes looked affectionately at his only child. Her dark brown hair was slightly windblown, and she had a smudge on her left cheek where she had wiped her hand after setting down the grocery sacks, but Rhodes thought she was one of the prettiest girls he'd ever seen. He wasn't far from wrong. Kathy's beauty had made her a real item with the young men of the town, and Rhodes wasn't sure he liked for her to be dating Johnny Sherman. Not that there was anything wrong with Johnny. It was just that Kathy was a wise and sensitive woman, and Johnny tended to think with his emotions. But maybe two like that could make a good match. Rhodes didn't really feel equipped to give advice on the subject, and he felt a twinge of unease. If only Claire were still alive. . . .

"What's the matter, Dad?" Kathy interrupted his thoughts. "Why're you looking at me with that blank stare."

Rhodes gave a rueful laugh. "Sorry, honey. Just woolgathering, I guess. Must be getting old."

Kathy walked to her father's side and gave him a quick hug. "You know better than that. You're looking younger every day. Why, not two minutes ago you had a call from that nice Mrs. Wilkie."

The grin that had formed on Rhodes's face changed to a frown and he gave a mock groan. "Not again."

Mrs. Wilkie was a widow of approximately Rhodes's age, by her own estimation. By Rhodes's estimation, she was at least ten years older. Not to mention about twenty pounds heavier, with brassy red hair that looked almost orange in the sun, a color that had never, Rhodes was sure, appeared in nature. Mrs. Wilkie was convinced that a year was a decent period of mourning and that the sheriff had already had a year. Now it was time for him to begin looking for a new wife, preferably herself.

"Yes, again," Kathy told him. "She wanted to remind you that tonight was the big night in Milsby."

This time Rhodes's groan was real. Mrs. Wilkie was the one who had asked him to appear tonight, so he had been certain that she would be there. But he'd allowed himself to forget that fact until now.

"I have too much on my mind today to have to face up to that woman," he said, rubbing his forehead.

"Yes," Kathy said. "I heard about poor Jeanne Clinton on the noon news. Any leads?"

"Just some suspicious characters. Ralph Claymore is going to chew me up over the whole mess tonight, no doubt about it. Your beau, Johnny Sherman, had the night tour through Thurston and didn't notice anything wrong in town. Hod Barrett's store was robbed, too."

Kathy put the last can of Green Giant corn in the metal cabinet and closed the door. "Well, he really can't say too much. It only just happened. No one expects you to solve it immediately. Besides, Mrs. Wilkie will be there to protect you."

"Even Mrs. Wilkie might not be able to help me out of this one," Rhodes said. "Do you have a date tonight?"

"Yes, Johnny's coming by and we're going to the early movie."

"Then I'll take a bath now. I don't want to be in your way when Johnny gets here. Just be sure not to keep him out past time for his shift to start."

Kathy didn't deign to answer, and Rhodes went into the bathroom.

As he soaked in the tub of lukewarm water, Rhodes wondered again if Kathy's staying in Clearview was the right thing. He'd been severely depressed when Claire died, but time had taken care of the worst of the pain. It wasn't easy getting used to the absence of a face and voice that you'd known intimately for twenty-five years. They'd married just after he'd gotten his associate of arts degree from Kingsley Junior College over in the next county, and she'd stayed with him through his brief stint as an officer on a big-city force, which he'd hated; through his jobs, both of them, as police chief in small towns; and through his tenure as sheriff of Blacklin County after his three years as chief in Clearview.

There were many county sheriffs, and Rhodes knew some of them, who were really politicians—men who liked the title, but not the job; men who turned all the work over to their deputies and spent their time in the drugstores drinking coffee with the rest of the good old boys. Men like Ralph Claymore. Rhodes had never been like that, and he never could be.

That meant that his job brought with it certain pressures, which could be smoothed over by a slick talker and dresser like Claymore but which Rhodes had to deal with through action. Claire had understood this and had understood that Rhodes would never keep regular hours, would always be on the job. There weren't many women who could have put up with his way of life, which was why so many of the good lawmen he knew were either divorced or separated from their wives.

And Claire had done a fine job with Kathy. If Claire were only here now, Kathy would be in the city in a job worthy of her talent instead of teaching in a small-town school. It was true that there were some fine young men in Clearview, and Johnny Sherman was probably one of them, but Dan had hoped for a better life for his only child.

As the bath began to relax him, Rhodes turned his mind to the problem of Jeanne Clinton. Bill Tomkins had found the body and hadn't hesitated to imply that Hod Barrett had an interest in the victim and had maybe visited her house after most folks in Thurston were long in bed. Could Tomkins be trying to shift suspicion? And Elmer had insisted almost too

28

strongly that his wife had had no visitors at all. Could it be that Elmer knew that his wife was fooling around and, instead of telling her to stop, had taken more certain measures? Elmer had punched in and out at work, but maybe he hadn't stayed there all the time. Rhodes thought he'd better check. And then there was Billy Joe Byron, and that bloody shirt. He wished he knew the blood type right now, but he'd bet that it was the same as Jeanne Clinton's. If it was, things didn't look so good for Billy Joe. Of course Hod Barrett didn't look any too clean either. He'd seemed awfully worried that Rhodes might talk to his wife.

Rhodes knew that he had a busy day ahead of him tomorrow, and then there was the forum that night. The forum reminded him of the attentive Mrs. Wilkie. He was going to have to do something about that woman, and do it soon. If it were at all possible she would rumor him into marriage with her. Too bad that Claymore was already married or Rhodes would have tried to switch her affections to his challenger. Claymore might have married her just to get her vote.

He knew that Claymore's little speech at the forum would be much better than his own. Rhodes rarely was able to express his real feelings about an issue, and the Jeanne Clinton thing would be impossible to comment on. Claymore would no doubt put a lot of emphasis on it. He hated to have to listen. The only good thing he could think of was that there would be lots of other candidates for other offices there, so the speeches would be mercifully short, by necessity. There was some comfort in that.

As his mind began to drift, he heard a car in the driveway. Then there was a knock on the door.

"Bye, Dad." He heard Kathy's voice call out. Then the door slammed and he was completely alone with his thoughts. By then the water was cold, so he pulled the stopper from the drain and stepped out on the mat, drying himself with the big, rough towel.

He thought about shaving, but then he thought again about Mrs. Wilkie and decided against it. No need to tempt fate.

4

MILSBY WAS NO longer really a town. It had been a town once, with stores, a barbershop, a drugstore, a bank, and even a movie theater. Now there was nothing left except a few scattered homes. The buildings that had formerly made up the town had all been demolished and the brick had been sold. The only structure of any size that remained was the schoolhouse, which was no longer really a school.

Milsby was, in fact, referred to these days as "the Milsby community" rather than as a town, and the old school served as the Milsby Community Center. Most of the residents who lived near the place remained fiercely loyal to the idea that they were part of a real geographical place on the map, and they tried to have as many activities in the school building as possible: community dances, bingo games (just voted in by the precinct, and as legal as marriage), church suppers, and candidates' forums with cake auctions.

Classes had long since disappeared from the former learning center. When the number of Milsby graduates per year had finally shrunk to one or two—three at most—the town fathers had realized that the tax burden was no longer worthwhile. They could consolidate their school district with Clearview's and save money. Their children would have to be bused, but that was a small sacrifice. Many of the local residents regarded the day of consolidation as a day of infamy, and it ranked right up there with December 7, 1941, as a topic of conversation whenever sneaky maneuverings were brought up. It was their impression that Milsby had begun to die the day the first students were bused to Clearview.

The town had begun to die long before then, of course, about the time that many of the men on surrounding farms found that they could make plenty of money just by putting their money in the soil bank and not farming a lick. Their families had nothing to tie them to the land, and they left for the delights of the big cities and easier jobs than the daylight-to-dark work required by farming.

But the old schoolhouse still remained. Built in the early part of the century of sturdy red brick, the building was not pretty at all. It was, however, serviceable. Despite the generations of careless youngsters that had subjected it to all kinds of abuse, its rooms still could be used for the activities of Milsby, especially the cafeteria, where the forum was to be held.

Rhodes pulled the county car into the dusty parking area and looked around for a good spot. He had deliberately arrived late, knowing that Ralph Claymore would do the same. At forums like this one, the candidates were not given an opportunity to speak according to the office for which they were running. Instead, as each one entered the building he was given a list to sign. The names were called from the list, the candidates speaking in the order in which they arrived. Claymore liked to arrive late, believing that speaking near the end gave him an advantage.

Rhodes didn't necessarily share Claymore's belief. He was pretty sure that nobody ever recalled a thing that any of the candidates said. He was convinced that the main purpose of the forum was to sell cakes, which wasn't a bad cause, since the money would go to the upkeep of the building. But on the off chance that Claymore was correct, Rhodes had decided to speak near the end also. At least there was the chance that he would get to speak after his opponent and answer any charges that were made, even if it wouldn't do much good.

Rhodes parked by a Trans-Am, owned no doubt, by one of the other candidates. Surely no one in Milsby drove such a car. He got out and walked to the back door of what had once

31

been the school boiler room, went through the room, and turned left into the hall where the cafeteria was located.

Mrs. Wilkie was waiting for him.

Her hair was spectacular. Rhodes was certain that he'd last seen a similar color and style worn by Carol Burnett in a skit parodying *The Little Foxes*. Otherwise, Mrs. Wilkie bore no physical resemblance to the svelte Ms. Burnett; tonight she had her formidable girth swathed in something resembling a Hawaiian tent.

"Why, good evening, Sheriff," Mrs. Wilkie cooed breathily. "You're just in time for the auction. But don't forget to sign in first." She handed him a yellow legal pad and a pen.

Rhodes was glad to see that Claymore's name was only one person above his own. "Good evening Mrs. Wilkie," he said. "You're looking mighty spruce tonight."

Mrs. Wilkie simpered and took back the legal pad.

Lord, Rhodes thought, what a man won't say to get himself elected.

"You just go on in, Sheriff, and have a seat with the other candidates," Mrs. Wilkie said. Rhodes started for the cafeteria door. "My cake's devil's food," she called after him in a stage whisper.

The cafeteria was brightly lighted by long fluorescent tubes. To Rhodes's left, the candidates sat in metal folding chairs lined up along the institutional-green wall. On the other side of the room, the Milsby crowd mixed and mingled in conversation. Rhodes didn't take a count, but it seemed likely that the crowd didn't outnumber the candidates by many. He turned to his left to look for a seat.

Ralph Claymore was sitting between a candidate named Peter Something-or-other, Rhodes couldn't recall, who was running for county clerk and Ivy Daniels, who was running for justice of the peace in precinct 4. The clerk candidate was stoutly built, with sandy hair, and in his navy blue suit he looked like a young senator more than a small-town boy. Rhodes had heard good things about him and hoped he'd win.

Ivy Daniels didn't look small-town either. Her short black hair had flecks of gray in it, but her tailored suit revealed the curves of a still youthful body. Naturally, Ralph Claymore was giving none of his attention to the young senator. He was talking animatedly to Ivy Daniels.

And he's a married man, Rhodes thought. Well, at least Ivy was unattached, or had been the last he'd heard. He wouldn't have minded talking to Ivy himself, but he didn't have too much time for that sort of thing. He walked over to the end of the row of chairs and sat next to Jack Parry, a candidate for county judge.

"Howdy, Sheriff," Parry said, putting out his hand. He was a big, folksy man, bluff and bald, with a full beard and a cigar always in his mouth—that or a dip of snuff.

Rhodes shook Parry's hand. "How you doing, Jack?" he said.

"Fine, but I'd a hell of a lot rather be having a quiet drink somewhere else right now. How about you?"

"Sure enough. Think we could have skipped out?"

Parry smiled around his cigar. "Not a chance. We might lose only a couple of votes from this crowd, but they'd tell everybody they know which ones of us didn't show up. No telling how many votes that would be."

Just as Rhodes was about to answer, a man walked to the front of the cafeteria to a makeshift podium fitted with a jury-rigged sound system. "Good evening, y'all," he said. On the second word, there was an electronic scream from the speakers near him, but it died away and he went on.

"I'm Jerry Bob Tyler, and I want to welcome ever' one of you to the annual Milsby cake auction and candidates' forum. I know you all look forward to hearing what the electioneers have to say just as much as I do"—which meant not at all, Rhodes thought—"but first we've got a real treat for you. Len and Belle are goin' to do a little of their famous pickin' and grinnin'."

Len and Belle tottered out from somewhere in the Milsby

crowd. Len, who looked to Rhodes to be about ninety years old, with a fringe of very white hair outlining a pink and liver-spotted skull, held a fiddle. Belle, just as old, and with almost as little hair, carried a mandolin. They stood tentatively by the podium for a second or two, they twanged a few strings. Seemingly satisfied, Len stamped his foot on the floor four times, and they broke into as spirited a rendition of "Soldier's Joy" as Rhodes had ever heard. It was hard to believe that the fingers of two people so old could be so nimble.

The crowd on both sides of the cafeteria began tapping their feet and clapping their hands in time with the music. The first song ended in a furious crescendo of fiddle and mandolin harmonies, and before anyone could draw a breath Len had stamped his foot again and begun "The Orange Blossom Special." By the time that one was over, the old man's head was completely red, and Belle's face wasn't much better. But they looked happy.

The old couple was replaced by a boy who looked like he might possibly be in the first grade. The guitar he carried was a cheap black Stella that almost hid him from the audience. Rhodes didn't catch his name; it sounded like "Tinker." Whatever his name was, the little boy knew three chords and sang "Sea of Heartbreak" in an alarming monotone that was just enough off key to set Rhodes's teeth on edge. Nevertheless, he got quite a round of applause.

"Ain't he cute?" Jerry Bob Tyler yelled over the crowd noise. "He's gonna be a real star someday, you mark my words." He raised his hands over his head and applauded loudly, the Milsby audience joining in with renewed fervor.

"Now then," Jerry Bob said when things had quieted. "It's time to get to a real important part of this evening's business. The big cake auction!" He waved his right hand to indicate the area behind him.

A few yards behind the podium, on the back wall, panels began to slide up. Where there had once been a serving table for the Milsby students there was now a counter loaded with cakes of all kinds: chocolate, angel's food, coconut, pineapple upside-down, devil's food, sheath, three-layer, and several kinds that Rhodes didn't even try to identify.

Jerry Bob walked back to the cakes and picked up one of the angel's food concoctions. "This here one's light as a feather, folks, handmade right from scratch if I know anything about cakes, and I'm an old cake eater from way back. What'm I bid on this little beauty?"

"Five dollars," called out the young senator-type, and the bidding was on.

When it was all over, Rhodes was the possessor of a devil's food cake for which he'd paid thirty-five dollars. He had no real idea what had made him bid on a devil's food cake, and he sincerely hoped that it wasn't Mrs. Wilkie's. She might expect him to drop by her house to cut it.

Then the speeches began. About the only one that held any interest for Rhodes, except for his own and Claymore's, was Ivy Daniels's. Women didn't usually run for the position of justice of the peace, and her opponent had made any number of subtle references to the fact that the JP was often called upon to leave the house at night, to be present at the scenes of sometimes gruesome accidents or even murders, and to perform other tasks that just weren't fit for a lady. Ivy didn't hesitate to counterattack. She felt that women were just as strong as men, and maybe stronger, she told the audience. She'd like to see any of the brave men she knew carry a baby for nine months and then deliver it. Then she'd know just how brave they really were.

Rhodes thought it was a good point, but most of the applause when Ivy sat down was merely polite, nothing more.

Ralph Claymore, when his turn came, looked more than ready. He'd already removed his hat, in deference to whatever old-fashioned ladies were still living—and there weren't many, because it was now quite common to see men who fancied themselves to be cowboys eating in any restaurant in Clearview while wearing a hat or a cap—but he still looked just like a sheriff should look. He was tall and slim, and his Levi's Saddleman jeans fit him to double knit perfection. His tapered western shirt had just the right amount of color in it, and his belt buckle tonight was a huge brass armadillo. He stood behind the podium as if he owned the building.

When he spoke, his voice was deep and pleasing. "I know that most of you people here know Dan Rhodes, my opponent in the sheriff's race," he began. "Well, I know him too, and like most of you I think he's done a fine job while he's been our sheriff. Not many fellows could have done half as well as he has. Why, I'd bet that violent crimes, crimes against persons, aren't up in our county by more than ten or twelve percent."

Nine point eight six percent, thought Rhodes, not counting Jeanne Clinton. Here it comes.

But it didn't come.

"Yep, Sheriff Rhodes has done real well. And the only reason that I'm here tonight is that I think I can do a little better. I'd like to see us have a new jail, for one thing. Not one that is a country club like those federal pens you read about, not one of those. Just a jail that doesn't have rats in it, and one that lets an accused man live like a man and not some kind of animal. I don't mean to treat the prisoners better than I'd treat some of you, but imagine what it might be like if your son or even your daughter got arrested for speeding and had maybe had a little too much to drink and had to spend a night in that jail we've got now. . . ."

Claymore went on, his voice deep and confident, his tone reassuring, while Rhodes's mind raced ahead unbelievingly. What was going on here? Claymore had a valid spot to attack him—the first murder in the county in nearly two years. But he wasn't saying a thing about it. Instead he was talking about things over which Rhodes had no real control. It was true that the sheriff could use his influence, whatever that might be, and it usually wasn't much, with the county commissioners; but that was all. The sheriff couldn't build the jail. He could staff it, see that it was run right and according to all the state and federal rules that were laid down. He could treat the prisoners fairly. He could see that they were fed properly and got the required exercise. Rhodes had always done this.

". . . And that's why I'm asking for your vote in the Democratic Primary on May 4," Claymore concluded. He smiled and dipped his head slightly to the applause.

Rhodes walked to the podium for his turn in a sort of daze. He had no idea what was going on here. True, there weren't many votes represented by this crowd, but a reporter from the Clearview *Herald* was in the audience. Claymore could have counted on a fair summary of whatever he said being in the next day's paper, and he said nothing that Rhodes wasn't going to refute easily.

Still thinking, Rhodes started to talk. "Friends, Ralph Claymore may think that he can do a better job than I can, but I sure don't." He said it positively but with a smile, and got a polite laugh in reply. "For one thing, the sheriff in this county doesn't have as much control over the building of a jail as you might think, or Mr. Claymore would have you believe. All that's up to your commissioners, and I think you'll find that they'll be reasonable about it." They had to be, he thought, considering what that judge had said.

"For my part," he went on, "I've always done my best to see that anybody who gets arrested in Blacklin County gets the fairest treatment possible. I don't think that any of you people here tonight have to worry about what might happen to any member of your family who got arrested on some minor charge, or even a major charge for that matter, because . . ."

Rhodes came to a stop then because he suddenly realized what was happening. He realized it even before he saw the little James Cagney look-alike getting up from where he'd been sitting inconspicuously in the back of the audience. Claymore had set him up.

Which meant that Claymore was both smarter and sneakier than Rhodes had given him credit for. Those two men had gotten out of jail only slightly earlier that day, and already Claymore had found them and gotten their stories.

It might not have happened that way, though, Rhodes realized. It was also possible that the men, or maybe only the one now getting up, had gone to Claymore. Maybe instead of filing a suit against the county, which they were almost certain to lose, they had decided to work with Claymore for a small payment out of his campaign funds. Either way, Rhodes knew that he was in for it.

The man had by now gotten to his feet and pushed to the front of the sparse crowd. "Sheriff, I'd like to ask you a little question," he said.

Mrs. Wilkie hurried over to cut him off, and for once Rhodes almost found himself liking her. But it was too late. Her frantic "No questions, no questions. This is not a debate . . ." was interrupted by the short man's voice cutting through like a table saw.

"I'd just like to ask the sheriff one thing," he said. "I'd like to know if it's a custom in all counties where the prisoners are treated well for the deputies to beat up on them for no reason." He pointed to his face, which even Rhodes had to admit looked pretty battered. Maybe even more battered than it had that morning. Good lord, Rhodes thought, could it be possible that Claymore had actually staged the whole thing? Could Johnny Sherman have been framed?

"That's right," the man went on, to the crowd now, "my buddy and I got whipped up on for no reason at all this morning, while we were just . . ."

"Wait a minute now," Rhodes said, his voice louder than he usually allowed it to get, which caused the makeshift mike to whistle and squeal once again. "Just hold on," he said in a normal tone. "You were arrested by a county officer in the course of his normal patrol. You were fighting with another man, and you refused . . ."

"That's bull, and you know it. You laws are all alike, and you stick together when it comes to something like this, but

38

we'll see. I'm going to sue you and that deputy of yours, and the whole county. Then people will know what things're really like in that jail of yours."

Then, before anyone realized what he was doing, the man turned and stalked the length of the cafeteria and out the door.

Rhodes made a few more remarks intended to assure his listeners that things weren't what they seemed, but there was so much buzzing of talk that he doubted they'd heard a word. Out of the corner of his eye he could see Claymore sitting in his chair, his legs crossed to show off his Tony Lama boots, a slight smile lingering on the corners of his mouth.

There was another fiddle player after that, but hardly anyone paid any attention. "I take it that this is hardly the high spot of your political career," Jack Parry whispered to Rhodes when he returned to his seat.

"You might say that," Rhodes said. "I guess it could be worse, though."

"Yeah," Parry said. "They might have caught you performing an unnatural act with the Baptist minister's wife in the choir loft."

Rhodes grinned. "Or with the minister himself," he said. "Even you'll have to admit that between him and his wife there's not much to choose."

"Too right," Parry said. "Well, I'm getting out of here before you get surrounded and questioned. Someone might think to ask me why the county judge is so friendly with a low-down skunk like you."

Rhodes saw that several of the people from the crowd were making their way toward him. He turned to answer them as best he could. At least, he thought, everything else was pretty much under control.

When the meeting finally broke up and Rhodes got back by the jail, they told him that Billy Joe Byron had escaped.

39

5

RHODES WAS NOT a man who lost his temper often. Most of the time he was, at least outwardly, in complete control of his emotions. This, however, was not one of those times.

"Goddammit," he exploded. "Billy Joe Byron hasn't got any more sense than a tame turkey! How in the hell could he escape? I just wish that someone would please explain that to me."

Hack Jensen was sitting by his radio looking sheepish, while old Lawton was taking the worst of Rhodes's anger. Lawton's smooth, unlined face was very red, and it looked as if he might cry at any minute. As the jailer, he was the one responsible for what had happened.

"I just don't understand it, Sheriff," Lawton said. "Maybe I'm gettin' too old for the job. I could have swore that everything was all right, but the door to his cell is wide open, like it wasn't ever locked. I fed Billy Joe about six-thirty, took his food right in like I always do for someone harmless like that, and I thought for sure I'd locked that door when I came out. Maybe I did, because he was still there when I picked up his tray at seven o'clock. That must be when I left the door open."

Rhodes suddenly felt sorry for the old man. They all thought that Billy Joe was a harmless prisoner. But what if he hadn't been? Or what if he wasn't? That blood test still hadn't come back.

"Why didn't you call me?" Rhodes asked. He didn't add that he would very much have appreciated being called away from the Milsby candidates' forum and cake auction. He hadn't mentioned what went on there.

"We would've put out a call, Sheriff," Hack said, "but we just found out Billy Joe was gone."

"Just found out?" Rhodes was puzzled.

"Yeah, he hasn't been gone long," Lawton said. "I checked the cells right before Johnny came in. Then when Johnny went out I checked again. He was gone then."

"Well, that's something. Is Johnny looking for him? He can't have gotten too far."

"Johnny said something about looking for him, but he figured that he couldn't look too long. Said he had to make his run."

"OK. I'll look for a while, too, but I'm going home and get some sleep if I don't find him pretty quick. I have a feeling that tomorrow's going to be a long day."

"They all are, lately," Hack said, and Lawton nodded in agreement.

It was nearly twelve o'clock when Rhodes drove up to Billy Joe Byron's shack. It was located on a dirt road about a mile out of town, not far from the former site of one of Clearview's sanitary landfills. Or dump grounds, to those less inclined to euphemism.

The shack had only one room and a narrow porch, and its roof sagged in the middle as if something huge had walked across it. The walls were scrap planks held together by rusty nails and covered with tar paper and shingles that Billy Joe had picked up at building sites after the houses were completed but before clean-up had begun. All around the house were scattered the remains of other people's trash that Billy Joe had scavenged in the years that the dump ground had been in operation—various mismatched leather shoes, their toes and soles curving upward, cracked and wrinkled from years of rain and sun; a headless plastic horse that had once been joined to a frame with springs; any number of aluminum lawn chairs, bent at crazy angles and missing all but a few tatters of their plastic webbing; glass bottles of all kinds; television picture tubes and empty radio cabinets; an exercise bicycle with no wheels.

"There's no place like home," Rhodes said aloud, to no one in particular. "Billy Joe," he called, "you in there?"

There was no answer, and Rhodes mounted the porch by means of a concrete block which served as a step.

There was a moon which gave quite a bit of light to the area around the house and lit up Billy Joe's trash collection with an eerie silver light, but the light didn't penetrate the interior of the house. It had been put together without the benefit of windows, and the low-hanging porch roof effectively cut off all illumination from the outside, in spite of the fact that there was no door.

"You'd have thought someone would have thrown away a door," Rhodes muttered. "Billy Joe! Come out if you're in there."

Again there was no response. Rhodes stepped through the empty doorway without hesitation, and the house fell in on him.

Or that's what it felt like, a sudden overwhelming crashing down on his head that sent him stunned and reeling through the dark. Something hit him again and he collapsed on the floor, struggled to rise, and then fell face down. He heard footsteps hollow on the porch, then the sound of a car engine.

Someone in here all the time, he thought. Car parked behind the house. He tried again to get up, but the effort was too much; he passed out.

When Rhodes woke up, his head hurt considerably. He reached to feel it, and his fingers immediately encountered a pulpy knot that felt like a baseball but that he knew probably wasn't that large. It was still very dark, so he knew that he hadn't been out long. He got unsteadily to his feet and walked carefully back out on the porch. Billy Joe Byron was standing by the county car.

"Well, I'll be damned," Rhodes said.

When he got Billy Joe back to the jail, Hack had gone home and Lawton was asleep in the little back room provided for him. It was just as well. He could hear the radio if any calls came in, but other noises didn't seem to register on him. Rhodes was able to get Billy Joe back to the cell without trouble.

All the way to the jail, Billy Joe had refused to speak. Rhodes had tried to get him to talk on any topic, but all Billy Joe did was shake his head and make gabbling noises. Rhodes was sure that it hadn't been Billy Joe inside the house, but if Billy Joe knew just who it had been, he wasn't about to tell. Rhodes had an aching head to convince him that whoever it was didn't intend to be gentle. He decided to go home and get a few hours sleep.

The next morning, Rhodes was back at the jail by the time Johnny Sherman got in at seven. "Any problems last night?" he asked.

Johnny shrugged. "Not a thing out of the ordinary that I could see. I paid pretty close attention in Thurston, you can bet on that."

"Any activity at all around Barrett's store?"

"Not that I noticed."

"Did you happen to notice whether Elmer Clinton's car was home? I didn't think he'd be at work," Rhodes said.

"I noticed. It was there around two."

Which meant that Elmer could have been out at Billy Joe's shack around twelve, Rhodes thought. "How about Barrett's car?" he asked.

"To tell the truth, I never noticed," Johnny said. "He has a garage on his house, I think, and keeps the doors down. No way to tell for sure. Why?"

"No reason, really. Just wondering." Rhodes wasn't ready yet to take anyone fully into his confidence. "You go on home and get some rest. I may have something for you later."

Johnny nodded and left just as Hack was coming in.

"Think we'll get the results of that blood test on Billy Joe's shirt today, Hack?"

The old man nodded. "Sure do. I told them lab boys to put on a real rush job, because this was a mighty important case for us. I'll bet we get the results this morning."

"Good. I'm afraid I already know what's going to show up, but I still want confirmation. I'm not sure what it's going to prove, though."

The truth was that Rhodes was convinced that Billy Joe was innocent of murder. His simple mind just didn't seem capable of the kind of violence that had been in evidence in Elmer Clinton's living room. That took a kind of derangement different from whatever went on in Billy Joe's head, but Rhodes wasn't sure just what kind of mind it took.

Too, Rhodes was still puzzled by the behavior of Ralph Claymore at the forum the night before. It was true that Claymore had scored heavily against him with the men in the audience, but he could have done even more damage, it seemed to Rhodes, if he had brought up Jeanne Clinton's death. It was always a bother to Rhodes when things didn't happen the way they should, and he was determined to find out what was going on. He was also determined to establish a link between Claymore and the former prisoner to see if he'd been set up.

The man's name was Terry Wayne, Rhodes learned by checking the arrest record. "Hack," he said, "get Buddy on the radio and tell him to check up on this Terry Wayne." He gave Hack Wayne's address. "Get him to talk to the neighbors and see what he can turn up. I especially want to know if Wayne knew Ralph Claymore, or if Claymore ever visited his house."

"Can do, Sheriff," Hack said.

44

Lawton came in from upstairs in the cell block. "See you got old Billy Joe back, Sheriff," he said sheepishly. "I'm sure sorry about leaving that cell door unlocked."

"This time, it's OK," Rhodes said. "Billy Joe's so harmless that no damage was done. But I hope it doesn't happen again."

Lawton shook his head. "You don't have to worry about that, Sheriff. I can promise that it won't. I'll be extra careful from now on."

"Fine. Now let's get to work."

"Work" consisted of routine complaints: a report that a man on the Milsby cut-off had seen a pickup with a canvas cover stopped by the road with a hand dangling from beneath the cover; a reported assault at the State Park; a robbery at the County Line Tavern. "Man says the driver of the pickup got out, walked around to the back, and stuck the hand under the canvas before he drove off," Lawton told Rhodes. "Probably just a couple of kids playing a joke. I gave the highway boys a description of the pickup, just in case."

The other problems were being routinely investigated by the deputies, so by mid-morning Rhodes was able to get on the road to Thurston. He planned to have a little talk with Mrs. Hod Barrett, among others.

"Yes, Sheriff," Mrs. Barrett said. "Hod was home all last night. I don't know where you think he might be going." She handed Rhodes a glass of iced tea with a few mint leaves stuck in it for flavor, then sat in a wicker rocker like the one she had already invited Rhodes to make himself at home in.

Rhodes had already thought of a story for that one. "I just thought that with these robberies around here he might be wanting to keep an eye on his store. I sort of got the idea that Hod didn't think we county boys were doing a very good job."

Mrs. Barrett took a sip of her own tea and said nothing. To Rhodes she seemed a fairly good-looking woman for her age, which he guessed at about fifty. A little dumpy maybe, and certainly her hair was almost totally gray, but no real reason there for Hod to be slipping over to the Clinton house. Of course, looks weren't everything, and some people at Hod's age just had to have a fling or two. Or at least give it a try. Rhodes decided to be more direct.

"Some folks also say that he and Jeanne Clinton had a liking for one another. That might give Hod a reason to be out looking around, maybe for whoever did it."

Mrs. Barrett looked at Rhodes with faded blue eyes. "Small-town gossip, Sheriff. That's all that is. You should know better than to trust anything like that."

"You're sure there's nothing to it, then?"

"Ask Hod, if you don't believe me."

"Oh, I believe you," Rhodes lied, taking a deep swallow of his drink. "That tea was mighty refreshing, Mrs. Barrett. I thank you."

"You're welcome," Mrs. Barrett said.

Hod Barrett was irate. "Sheriff, you come in here, interrupt my business, cause me to lose money, and then pull some outrageous lie like that out of the air, why it's enough to make a man downright mad. If you weren't an officer of the law, I'd throw you right out that door!"

"It's no lie, Hod. Your car's been seen over there," Rhodes said. It hadn't, but as long as he was being accused of lying he might as well try a little. The two men were in the little back storeroom of Barrett's store, standing behind a three-high stack of boxes of Northern toilet tissue, the only place in the store where there was any privacy.

"No way! No way!" Barrett's hair seemed to bristle even more than usual. "I never drove . . ." He stopped himself, shoved his fists into his pockets, and turned away.

"You never drove," Rhodes said softly, "but you walked. People in town know, Hod. I think your wife knows, too."

Barrett leaned tensely forward and whipped his fists out of

his pockets, waving them futilely in the dim light of the storeroom. Rhodes wondered just how much damage those fists could do to a woman if Barrett were angry enough to attack her.

"I didn't tell her, Hod," Rhodes said. "I don't think anyone told her. Women just know things like that."

Barrett sat down abruptly on a case of canned pineapple chunks. "You don't know what it's like, Sheriff," he said in a strangely subdued voice. He hung his head and looked at the grimy, cracked concrete floor, worn smooth and black with the years of boxes being piled and moved and slid across it. Somewhere above, a fly buzzed as it looked for a way out.

"I haven't slept with my wife for three years," Barrett said. "I'm not sure what the problem is; she's not the kind of woman you can talk to about things. I sort of tried, at first. I even tried to get her to go to that new woman's doctor over in Clearview. It didn't do any good."

Rhodes said nothing. Barrett clasped his hands and studied them intently. The buzzing of the fly died away as it found a crack in the wall.

After a minute Barrett went on. "Jeanne Clinton came to the store a lot, she was friendly. You know. Not flirting, just friendly. I liked her, and she liked me too, I think. Anyway, it had gotten so that I was taking a walk at night, just to get out of the house. One night I saw the Clintons' light on."

"You mean you saw Jeanne's light on," Rhodes said. "You knew that Elmer worked at night."

"This wasn't that late," Barrett said. "Elmer was still there. I just went up to the door and knocked. They invited me in and we talked awhile. Harmless talk." He paused again.

"And that's all there was to it?" Rhodes said.

"Naw, that's not all. That was all at first, but then I got to waiting a little later to take my walk. After Elmer had gone."

"How long had this been going on?"

"A few months, that's all." Barrett's voice began to regain its vehemence. "But there was nothing shameful about what I did there, Sheriff. Jeanne Clinton was a fine girl, not the kind to do anything wrong. Sure, she let me in after her husband had left, but all we ever did was talk. She had a way of talking that made me forget what was wrong at home; she made me laugh.''

Rhodes was skeptical. "Did Elmer know you were visiting over there after he went to work?"

"Probably not," Barrett said, quiet again. "We weren't doin' anything wrong, but he might not have understood that. There was no harm in him not knowing."

Rhodes had several doubts about that, but he had another question to ask. "How about the night she was killed, Hod?"

"I swear to God, Sheriff, I had nothing to do with that! I've told you the truth. Surely you couldn't believe that I . . ."

"I'm not saying what I believe or don't believe, Hod. What I want you to tell me is if you were over at the Clintons' house the night she was killed."

Barrett's answer was interrupted by a voice calling from the main part of the store. "Hod! You better get out here. You got customers linin' the walls! Some of 'em want to check out!"

Rhodes walked around the toilet tissue boxes and stuck his head out the storeroom door. "He'll be out in just a minute, folks. Hod's store got robbed the other night, and I have to conduct an investigation." He went back to where Barrett sat on the pineapple.

"Well, Hod?"

Barrett nodded wearily. "Yeah, Sheriff. Yeah. I was there."

He'd gone over about twelve-thirty, maybe a little earlier, made the usual jokes with Jeanne about his insomnia (the reason he gave for being out walking so late; he'd never told the real one), had a soft drink, and walked back home.

"That's all it was, Sheriff. That's all it ever amounted to. We'd just talk, have a Coke, and I'd go home. I never laid a hand on her, never."

"And your wife knew about this?"

"I don't know. I've been sleeping in the spare bedroom for

so long, I don't even know if she was awake. She goes to bed and reads her Bible and turns off the light pretty early. I think she's been asleep when I've left the house."

Rhodes thought for a minute. "All right, Hod. You go on out there and wait on your customers. I haven't got any reason to hold you now. Just don't think about making any trips to Mexico in the near future."

Barrett got up and started out of the storeroom. "I'm not going anywhere, Sheriff. But I didn't kill Jeanne. And I didn't rob my own store. You forget that there was more than one crime here in Thurston that night?"

"No, Hod, I haven't forgotten. And if you're thinking that there might be a connection between them, you may be thinking right. We'll see. I may be slow, but I usually get the job done."

Barrett had recovered some of his antagonism. "Save that for the campaign speeches," he said. "I go by results, myself."

So do I, thought Rhodes, so do I; I just wish I had some.

It was shortly after noon when Rhodes got back to Clearview, so he drove by his house for a sandwich and a glass of milk. Attached to the door of the refrigerator by a magnet that looked something like a pregnant ladybug with red wings and a black head was a note from Kathy, written in her precisely formed characters:

"Ivy Daniels called this morning before I left for school. She wants you to call her back when you get a chance. She didn't leave any other message. Think she wants a date?" There was a phone number at the end.

Rhodes smiled at his daughter's question. It was hardly likely that Ivy Daniels wanted a date with him. She probably had a busy enough social life without having to look for men on her own.

He wondered what she did want, though. Maybe it had something to do with what had happened at Milsby last night.

Rhodes opened the refrigerator and got out a plastic jug of low-fat milk, a package of thin-sliced bologna, and a jar of Gulden's mustard. He'd hoped for a slice of cheese, but there was none in the usual spot. Kathy had forgotten to buy it. He made a sandwich with wholewheat bread and poured a tall glass of the milk.

After he ate, he would call Ivy Daniels.

6

AFTER IVY DANIELS'S husband had died in an automobile accident in another state, she'd immediately found a job. The husband had been a salesman of farm implements, had earned a good salary, and had been well insured; but Ivy was not the type of woman to sit around the house and live off insurance payments. She had an active mind and wanted to feel useful, which was also why she was running for justice of the peace.

Finding a job had been easy. She had happened to remark to Stan Pence, the owner of the independent insurance agency who had handled her husband's policies, that she would like to go to work. Pence, who had been looking for a second secretary, hired her virtually on the spot. Ivy had been working for Pence for three years, and he secretly hoped that she would lose her political race. He would have a very hard time finding someone to replace her, because her efficiency and quick intelligence had made her almost indispensable to his office.

The office was where Rhodes reached her after he finished his lunchtime sandwich. "My daughter left a note asking me to call," he explained after the first secretary had put him through to Ivy.

"Yes," she said. "I . . . I don't really know how to put this, Sheriff, but it's related to what happened at the forum last night."

There was a pause.

"Well," Rhodes said, "sometimes it's best just to come right out and say what's on your mind."

"That's true, but since I called earlier, I've thought it over. It's not something I'd like to discuss on the phone."

What do you know? thought Rhodes. Maybe she does want a date after all. But he didn't say it. "If that's the case, maybe we could get together after you get off work," he said, and stopped. He found himself almost embarrassed. It had been quite a while since he had talked to a woman about meeting him after work. In fact, he'd never done it. The idea of the date began to grow in his mind, and he found himself feeling more and more like an adolescent. He glanced down to make sure that he wasn't digging his toe into the rug. Why should a simple conversation with Ivy Daniels affect him this way?

He ended the awkward silence by saying, somewhat to his surprise, "I could pick you up about seven. We could have dinner."

"Why that's a very nice idea, Sheriff," Ivy Daniels said brightly. It was clear that she was a little surprised herself.

"Don't dress up," Rhodes said quickly. "I mean, don't . . ."

"I understand, Sheriff. A man in your position wouldn't have time for anything fancy."

"Uh, it's not that. It's, well, never mind. We'll go to Jeoff's. Is that all right?"

"That would be very nice. I'll see you at seven, then."

"Yes, seven," Rhodes repeated and hung up the phone. He wondered what he might be getting himself into.

At the jail that afternoon, Hack had the report on the bloodstains on Billy Joe Byron's shirt. "Type A," he said. "Same type as Jeanne Clinton."

"And Billy Joe?" Rhodes asked.

"Plain old type O, is what our records show."

"That's what I was afraid of," Rhodes said. He sat down in a rickety desk chair. There might be all kinds of good reasons why Billy Joe had type A blood on his shirt, or there might not. Could Billy Joe be a murderer? To Rhodes it just didn't seem possible. Billy Joe might peep in a window, but he wouldn't hurt a fly.

"What do you think, Hack?" he asked.

"I ain't the sheriff," Hack said. "I don't get paid enough to do any thinkin'."

"Pretend you're getting a bonus this year."

"In that case, I might think that it just don't seem possible that a harmless sort of a fella like Billy Joe could murder somebody like Jeanne Clinton. Seems like if somebody like her told him to go away and leave her alone, he'd just go away and not say another word."

Rhodes was glad to see that his own instincts weren't too far out of line with Hack's. "I feel exactly the same way," he said, "but just the same we better hang on to Billy Joe for a few days. I don't believe any lawyer is going to come around worrying about his civil rights, and it's barely possible that he's guilty. I wish he'd talk to us, but if he won't I'll just keep looking for answers somewhere else."

"Fine with me," said Hack. "Another thing. Buddy came in and told me to let you know that as far as he can establish there's no connection a'tall between Terry Wayne and Ralph Claymore."

Rhodes shook his head. "OK, but tell him to keep on looking. Something funny's going on there."

"Right," Hack said, picking up a slip of paper from in front of his radio. "Now there's a few other things I need to ask you about."

"Such as?"

"Such as Ella Conner."

Rhodes groaned. "The ducks?"

"You guessed it," Hack said, smiling. Ella Conner started calling every spring, as regular as the change of season, about her neighbor's ducks, which she felt were illegally harvesting her garden spot.

"Did you send anybody around?" Rhodes asked.

"Sent Buddy. He run the ducks back home. Ella wanted

him to shoot one or two of them for what Buddy says she called an 'object lesson.' "

"Lord, I hope Buddy had more sense than to do something like that."

"He did, but if I was you I wouldn't be countin' on Ella's vote this time around. Old Man Evans's either, come to that. He was pretty mad about Buddy chasin' his ducks." At the thought of the deputy pursuing the criminal ducks, Hack laughed aloud.

Rhodes tried to manage a smile, but he wasn't able. It was almost too much. Murder wasn't bad enough. Now he'd lost two votes because of ducks in Ella Conner's garden spot.

"Then there's this guy upstairs," Hack said.

"What guy upstairs?"

"The Polish refugee," Hack said, clearly enjoying himself.

"You're kidding," Rhodes said. He was actually surprised. This was a new one on him.

"Not kidding a bit," Hack said. "Picked him up out on 77, walking the median stripe. What do they drink over there in Poland? Besides water, I mean?"

"Vodka, these days," Rhodes told him.

"Yeah. Well, this guy must have drunk about ten bottles of the stuff."

"Can he speak English?"

"Some. Enough to say he's a Polish refugee. Why, you goin' to question him?"

"I thought I might," Rhodes said.

"Wouldn't do you no good right now," Hack said. "He's snorin' so loud, you couldn't hear what he said."

"We'll check him out later then," Rhodes said. He changed the subject. "Tell me, Hack. What do you know about Bill Tomkins?"

Hack thought for a second or two. "He's the fella found Jeanne Clinton's body, right?"

"Right. You know much about him?"

"Not a lot, and that's the truth. I don't know too many folks over in Thurston. I hear he don't work for a livin', though. Supposed to have some kind of a disability pension from the government."

Rhodes thought about Tomkins and his breathing problem. Maybe that was the reason for the pension.

"Ever hear anything about him and Jeanne?"

"Not a thing, and from all I've heard lately that Jeanne was a mighty nice girl. Maybe a little wild when she was younger, but not a bit of it anymore. Marryin' old Elmer seems to have calmed her down a whole lot. Anything about her and Bill Tomkins, well, I expect you'd have to ask around over in Thurston for something like that."

"That's what I plan to be doing," Rhodes said. But that will have to wait until tomorrow, he thought. He already had his evening planned; even a good sheriff couldn't devote his whole life to the job.

He didn't mention his meeting with Ivy Daniels to Hack. Hack might interpret it as a date instead of as a meeting with an informant.

That evening, Kathy was careful not to make any remarks about her father's plans. She was privately of the mind that it was time he started having a little social life, but that wasn't the kind of thing he would like to have her say.

Rhodes bathed and dressed in a sport shirt and slacks. It felt strange not to have on his badge and twill uniform. It felt even stranger not to have his .38 caliber Police Special hanging on his belt. He didn't particularly like to carry it, but people expected it of him, so he did. Now, without it, he felt slightly unbalanced, as if he might tip over backwards and fall.

"I understand that Jeoff's is a pretty fancy place," he said to Kathy, who was sitting in the kitchen at the round oak table with a stack of ruled papers in front of her.

Kathy put down her red pen, moved the papers aside, and looked at her father. "Fancy for Clearview, maybe," she said. "That's about all you can say for it. But the food's not bad."

"You can get wine there," Rhodes said, half questioningly.

"Yes, but you have to be a member of their private 'club.' That just means that you pay the waitress a five-dollar fee, and she gives you a card with your name and membership number on it. Then you can order wine any time you go for a year."

"I don't know very much about ordering wine."

"Just ask for the house wine. It's not bad, and you can get it by the glass instead of by the bottle."

"You've been there, I take it." Rhodes was not really surprised.

"Sure. Where else is there to go if you want a good meal and a pleasant atmosphere?" Kathy picked up her pen and started looking over the top paper. "It's very popular."

"Yeah, well, I guess I'm just not used to this sort of thing," Rhodes said ruefully. "I'm too old to be taking a strange woman out to dinner." He glanced down at his stomach and was dismayed that he couldn't quite see his belt buckle. "I don't know why I didn't just go by her house and see what she wanted to say. Sometimes I just talk before I think about what I'm getting myself into."

Kathy stood up and kissed her father on the cheek. "Don't be silly. It'll do you good to get away from your problems and have a nice dinner with an attractive woman."

Rhodes had to laugh. "It almost seems as if you'll be glad to get rid of me. You sound like you want me out of the house."

"That's not it at all. Just enjoy yourself and don't worry so much."

"I'll try," Rhodes said, not making any promises.

Jeoff's was on a side street just off a main thoroughfare. It was actually a remodeled private home, with tables in the various rooms. There was a green, tree-shaded yard, which was crossed by a sidewalk. To obtain entrance, customers had to ring the doorbell, which was answered by a young waitress dressed as if she might be about to set off for school. It was all a little too cute for Rhodes's taste, but Ivy Daniels seemed to like it.

"Look at all the plants," she said as Rhodes held her chair for her. "They've really done a nice job with them."

It was true. The room in which they had been seated looked to Rhodes like a miniature jungle. The walls were hung with baskets of green plants, and not a corner was bare of something growing. In fact, the room was so small that there was room only for the one table and all the plants. Rhodes liked the privacy, but he wasn't overly fond of the plants.

"They're all right," he said. "It's the skylight that does it." In remodeling the house, the restaurant owners had installed a sizeable skylight in each of the dining rooms.

Rhodes walked around the table to his own seat, brushing a Boston fern with his leg. The waitress came in, and he paid her five dollars to join the 'club.'

"What wine can I get you?" the waitress asked, after Rhodes had slipped his new identification card into his billfold.

"What are the house wines?" Rhodes asked, feeling sophisticated.

"We have a white wine and a rosé," the waitress said.

"Which would you prefer, Ivy?" Rhodes asked. They had decided on first names while driving over.

"The rosé, please," she said.

"I'll have the same," Rhodes said.

The waitress left them with menus, and Rhodes glanced covertly at Ivy while choosing his meal. He had to admit that he liked what he saw, a good, strong face, not exactly pretty, but certainly handsome. Her hair was short and seemed to accent her features in just the right way, softening them slightly. Her eyes were blue, and her teeth were even and straight.

But what does it matter? Rhodes thought. I'm not really interested. "What looks good to you?" he asked.

"The small tenderloin, I think. Well done," she added.

"Sounds good to me too. I'm glad I won't have to watch the blood when you cut."

I've got to do better than that, Rhodes thought, even if I'm not interested.

But Ivy seemed not to notice anything crude in his statement. "I'll have the salad, not the soup, and a baked potato instead of the French fries," she said.

"So far, so good," Rhodes said. "I'll have the same thing."

The waitress came with the wine and took their orders. After she had gone, Rhodes decided that it was time to find out why Ivy Daniels had wanted to talk to him. He took a sip of the wine, which wasn't too bad, although he didn't really like wine, and said, "I was a little surprised to get your call. Were you that impressed with me last night?"

Ivy smiled. "It does have to do with last night," she said, "but not necessarily with my impression of you."

"You weren't impressed, then?"

"Oh, I was impressed, all right, but I was more impressed with that stunt of Ralph Claymore's. I thought it was quite unfair."

The waitress came back in with the salads and a basket of breadsticks and crackers, along with a revolving stand holding various kinds of dressing. Ivy helped herself to the Thousand Island, as did Rhodes. Then he took a breadstick and unwrapped it. "I don't think that what happened was entirely Claymore's fault," he said. "I've done a little checking, and I'm pretty sure that he and Terry Wayne—the guy who made the big scene—don't know one another."

"Oh," Ivy said. "I was so sure that it was a setup."

"I didn't say it wasn't a setup. I agree with you that it was. I'm just saying that I don't think it was Claymore's idea. I think that Wayne probably went to him with it."

"But he went along with Wayne."

"Well, you can't blame him, really. It was a ready-made piece of sensation."

"Yes, and it made the front page of this afternoon's paper."

Rhodes usually read the paper after eating supper, and in

his rush to pick up Ivy he had forgotten all about it. "Is that so?" he said.

"It's so. The paper didn't really take sides, but it didn't look so good for you."

They ate in silence for a minute. They both knew that the Clearview paper rarely took sides in any election.

Finally, after mastering a particularly large piece of lettuce, Rhodes said, "I'll bet you didn't call just to offer me your sympathy."

"That's right, I didn't. I don't really know how to go into this. It's just that I didn't like what happened, and I know something that probably you should know. But it may not be important at all, and I don't like to think that I'm being vindictive by telling you. Besides . . ."

"Hold on, hold on," Rhodes said. "The best thing to do is just to tell me. Then we'll work on the morality of it. It's too late to hold back now."

"Couldn't we just have a nice dinner and talk about something else?"

Rhodes suddenly realized how much he was enjoying talking to this woman, and he knew that he really didn't care if she had anything of importance to tell him or not. But he said, "I think that you should go ahead and tell me. You wanted to, or you wouldn't have called. We can have another dinner later and talk about something else at it."

Ivy looked at him. "That would be very nice. The other dinner, I mean. I think I'd like that." She paused and took a sip of wine. "Now. What I wanted to tell you was this. I have an aunt who lives in Thurston. She told me yesterday afternoon that Ralph Claymore has been visiting Jeanne Clinton."

So that's why he avoided that topic last night, Rhodes thought. He didn't want to be tied to it in any way. "How does she know?" he said.

"Someone told her, she said."

"Did she say who it was?"

"Yes. Someone named Bill Tomkins."

7

IT WAS FRIDAY morning, the morning that most residents of Blacklin County looked forward to each week. But that was not the case in the sheriff's department. Friday meant that the weekend was coming, the weekend when ordinary citizens would be getting ready to go to the lake and do a little fishing, go to the local clubs and do a little drinking, go out on the highway and blow the carbon out of their car's engine. For some other citizens, not so ordinary, it meant a chance to sneak in a not-so-carefully-guarded store or get up a friendly little game of poker in an abandoned warehouse or maybe just drive off from a convenient self-service gas station without paying.

The latter types the sheriff's department would always have with them, and to tell the truth Rhodes and his deputies didn't even spend very much time worrying about them. They had to worry about the ordinary folks, the ones whose boats hit a snag in the lake and disappeared under the brownish water; the ones who got a little too excited when their girlfriends won a wet T-shirt contest and strangers, who had to be disciplined, looked at them too long and hard; the ones who were out endangering everyone else's lives by zooming down the county roads at ninety miles an hour.

Thursday night, however, had been quiet; Hack had little to report when Rhodes came in. "Just a couple of drunks, and one little domestic fight. Billy Joe's doing fine. Him and that Polish fella have hit it off right well."

"Just how do you mean that?" Rhodes said.

"I mean they don't bother one another none. Billy Joe still

ain't talking, and the Polish fella can't talk so any of us can understand him. Except that Bob says he ain't Polish. He's gonna check up on him today."

"Well, keep me posted," Rhodes said. "I'll be back this afternoon."

"Thurston again?"

"That's right. Thurston again." Rhodes left the office.

April was Rhodes's favorite month, even in election years. It might have seemed a cruel one to that poet Kathy had once told Rhodes about. T. S. Eliot, that was his name. Old T. S. hadn't been from Texas, though, to see the way the grass and wildflowers just seemed to spread all over the place almost overnight if the rains were right. It was a pleasure to drive along and look at things growing.

Unfortunately, the pleasure was marred considerably by the thoughts that kept crowding themselves into Rhodes's mind, thoughts not connected in any way with the freshness of the season. There was Ralph Claymore, for one thing. It was beginning to seem as if everyone in Blacklin County had been slipping around to see Jeanne Clinton on the sly, even Claymore, who therefore almost certainly had to be considered a suspect in her murder.

And there was Billy Joe, with what was probably Jeanne's blood on his shirt. Not to mention Hod Barrett, who certainly had the physical equipment to do the job, not to mention the temperament. Of course, if you wanted a motive, you couldn't forget Elmer.

But it was Bill Tomkins who was worrying Rhodes the most right now. Tomkins hadn't minded at all mentioning the fact that Hod Barrett was seeing Jeanne, or if he'd minded, it hadn't taken much to get him to mention it. But he'd held back about Claymore. Why? That was the main thing Rhodes wanted to ask him. Besides, if he'd held out one bit of information, he might have held out more. What if he'd been stopping in at Elmer's himself? He seemed to be about the only one who hadn't been, if what Rhodes had found out about Claymore was true.

Thinking about how he'd gotten that piece of news turned Rhodes's mind into channels of thought that were considerably more pleasant, if still somewhat puzzling and complicated. He hadn't really thought of women at all, as *women,* since the death of his wife. He'd dealt with women on both sides of the law, seen them at stores and in restaurants, talked to them in the course of his re-election campaign (such as it was); but he had not until the night before thought of one of all those women—certainly not someone like Mrs. Wilkie—as being of a different sex from him. It was as if he had been neutralized in some way, had lost his sexual feelings completely.

Now he realized that those feelings hadn't been lost. They'd just been in mourning, or storage, or hibernation, or wherever it was that such things went after the death of a wife that you'd loved long and deeply. Now, stirred by Ivy Daniels, they were back.

Rhodes wasn't sure just what the attraction was that she held for him. She was a good-looking woman, of course. There was that. But there was more to it. There was something about her that he liked: her self-sufficiency, her competence, something like that. Anyway, he thought, it did no good to try to explain it; the feeling was there, and that was that. What he would do about it was something else again.

Last night he had taken her home and walked her to her door. There was no adolescent heavy breathing, no panting good-night kiss on the order of the latest romance novel's description; yet both of them knew that there was something between them, a feeling that neither was quite ready to acknowledge in words but which was nevertheless obviously present.

Rhodes had followed through on his earlier hint, to which Ivy had responded so positively, and asked her to have dinner with him again. They would be going out Saturday night. He

62

found himself wondering whether he should buy a sports jacket for the occasion. He hadn't had much need to dress up lately.

Well, he wouldn't worry about it yet. Maybe they could just go somewhere and get a hamburger. Ivy looked like the kind of woman who didn't demand that you make a big impression on her. Besides, they'd already been to the fanciest restaurant in Clearview. It was all downhill from Jeoff's.

Rhodes's pleasant thoughts were interrupted by his arrival in Thurston. The town was clearly dying, and before long it would probably go the way of Milsby. There was only one paved street, and that was actually a farm-to-market road leading on to another little town. The only businesses left in Thurston were on the paved street—Hod Barrett's grocery, the post office (the only new building in town), the bank, a hardware store, a tavern ("beer joint" the residents called it), another grocery store even smaller than Barrett's. There had been other stores once, but they were now almost forgotten. A local resident had bought their buildings, torn them down, and sold the brick. On graveled streets and dirt roads leading off the paved one were the homes and churches.

Looking at one of the latter off to his right, the First United Methodist Church, a white frame structure with a black shingle roof badly in need of replacement, Rhodes happened to think of Barrett's remark about his wife. "She goes to bed and reads her Bible. . . ." That was what Hod had said. Thinking about it, Rhodes decided to pay Mrs. Barrett another call, even before he visited Bill Tomkins.

The Barrett house wasn't like every other house in Thurston. It was what Rhodes's mother used to call "spruce." It was more than that; it was immaculate. Funny he hadn't really noticed that the first time. The lawn looked as if it had been edged with a ruler. The bushes might have been trimmed by an artist; there was not a single twig above the proper level. There wasn't even a leaf out of place, for that matter.

Rhodes remembered Hod's standard joke about buying his wife the best yard equipment money could buy. She certainly deserved it; she knew just how to use it.

As Rhodes parked his car in the drive, he noticed that Mrs. Barrett's passion for order extended beyond her lawn. Rhodes had heard of houses that were so clean you could eat off the floor—the Barrett house was so clean that he had no doubt you could eat off the driveway. He recalled the spic-and-span room he had sat in before, the coaster he had been provided for his glass of tea. Mrs. Barrett was a woman whose desire for cleanliness and order was far out of the ordinary. He wondered just how far that passion did extend.

When she answered his knock at the door, Mrs. Barrett was wearing a plain housedress. Her hair was caught up in a sort of turban fashioned from a faded pink towel, and she held a brush in one hand.

"Oh, it's you again, Sheriff," she said. "I was just cleaning the light fixtures." She gestured with the brush. "Sometimes I take them down and wash them in the bathtub, but I thought they could go for another week without that."

Rhodes wondered vaguely if his own light fixtures had ever been washed in the bathtub. He was pretty certain that they hadn't even been dusted since his wife's death, unless Kathy had done it and not mentioned it to him. Somehow, he didn't think that had happened.

"I was in town to see someone else," Rhodes said, "and I thought of a few more questions that I wanted to ask you." He paused. "If it wouldn't be too much of an interruption."

Mrs. Barrett looked at him calmly. "I suppose not," she said, stepping back from the doorway and holding the screen door open for him.

She asked Rhodes to have a seat, but she didn't offer to bring him any tea. "I'm really very busy, Sheriff. There's a lot of cleaning to be done in a house this size, though most people wouldn't think so. I hope this won't take too long."

"No," Rhodes said. "Not too long. You see, I was talking

64

to Hod the other day, and he told me that you and he were . . . well . . . having some sort of difficulty. He seemed to me to imply, even if he didn't really say it, that the problem might have something to do with your religious beliefs."

Mrs. Barrett's back stiffened, though Rhodes wouldn't have thought that it could have gotten any stiffer than it already was. He was sorry to have to talk about these things with her. He was small-town enough to dislike some of the things he had to do, but that had never stopped him from doing them.

"I don't know what you mean," Mrs. Barrett said. "Of course I'm a believing woman, but so should we all be believers."

She wasn't going to make it easy, Rhodes thought. "What I mean is," he said slowly, "what I mean is that he seemed to imply that you read your Bible an awful lot, even at night. That you . . . uh . . . that you even read it in the bed."

That was as much of a hint as Rhodes was going to allow himself, but Mrs. Barrett got it. Her face turned almost as red now as her husband's had been on the morning Rhodes had been investigating the robbery of his store, just before Jeanne Clinton's body had been found. And for the same reason. Mrs. Barrett was filled with what she would no doubt have called "righteous anger."

"I don't believe that when or where I read my Bible is any business of yours, Sheriff Rhodes," she said in the same tone an elementary teacher might use to scold a particularly troublesome pupil.

"Generally speaking, I'd agree with that," Rhodes told her. "But this isn't a general thing. Some bad things have been happening here in Thurston lately, and some of them seem to involve your husband. So I try to find out about things that will help me do my job."

"I can't believe that." Mrs. Barrett's hand gripped the handle of her brush so hard that the knuckles whitened. It was a strong hand.

"It's true enough, though," Rhodes said. "Hod could even be in trouble."

Mrs. Barrett looked down at her immaculate rug. "All right," she said in a furious voice, her head shaking. "All right."

Rhodes said nothing.

Finally Mrs. Barrett looked up, more in control of herself now. When she spoke, her voice was firm and had a stern, lecturing tone. "Marital relations, Sheriff Rhodes, are meant for the purpose of having children, creating a family. I had always hoped to have children of my own, but we never did, Hod and I. Then I had to have an operation. After that, a family wasn't possible. Do you understand?"

Rhodes shook his head affirmatively, though he wasn't sure he did. Did she think that he might not know about hysterectomies? Or did she think he might not understand about a family?

Mrs. Barrett, however, accepted the head shake and continued the lecture. "The Bible tells us that marriage—and what goes with it—is for the purpose of being fruitful, of bringing issue into the world. If you can't do that, then . . . relations are unnecessary. Oh, there are those"—her voice began to rise—"there are those, I know there are those, who use the flesh for other means, who defile the purity of the flesh for pleasure, but they shall have their reward! They shall be purified in the refiner's fire! They shall . . ."

She stopped suddenly to look at Rhodes. The room seemed to echo with her voice.

"I see what you mean," Rhodes said. For the first time he was getting a glimpse of Mrs. Barrett's fervor, and he was beginning to understand why Hod went out walking. "Does your husband feel the same way?" he asked.

Mrs. Barrett spoke in her lecturing tone once more. "I'm afraid that Hod is not a purely Christian man," she said. "He tries to be, I think, but he won't go to my church with me. The

Devil still has a little bit of a hold on him. He feels the call of the flesh, but that sin will be on his own head, not mine."

Rhodes wondered about the church Mrs. Barrett must attend, but he didn't ask. Instead he said, "Do you think Hod's need for 'the flesh' might cause Hod to stray from the right path?" He might not be in the congregation of Mrs. Barrett's church, but his upbringing had prepared him to talk to people like her in their own language.

"Hod has made errors in this life, Sheriff, as we all have, but I do not believe that he has strayed that far. Oh yes, I know what you must be thinking. You think that maybe he visited that floozie Jeanne for carnal pleasure. I could tell that you had that very thought in mind from the beginning." Her voice was cold now, cold as one of the blue northers that swept down on Thurston from the Panhandle in January. "But I don't believe he did. Surely he would not dare to transgress God's law so openly."

Rhodes stood up, and Mrs. Barrett immediately walked to the chair in which he had been sitting, straightening the antimacasser on the plump back.

"Well," Rhodes said, "I guess that's all for now Mrs. Barrett. You did know that Hod was going out at night, though?"

"Of course I knew, Sheriff, but I never said anything. A man may be a born deceiver, but sooner or later he deceives no one but himself."

"That's not from the Bible, is it?" said Rhodes as he stepped to the door and opened it.

"No," Mrs. Barrett said. "No, that's not from the Bible. That's from me."

As he drove away from the Barrett house, Rhodes thought again about Ivy Daniels. He hoped she didn't feel like Mrs. Barrett, and he was pretty sure that she didn't. He and Claire had shared a very satisfying sex life both before and after the birth of Kathy, and he had never seen anything irreligious about that.

In a matter of seconds he was back on Thurston's main street, and he parked at Hod's store. He got out and went in. Hod was sacking groceries and didn't look up, so Rhodes stepped to the loafer's bench. "Bill Tomkins been in today?" he said.

Larry Bell bent over and spit into his styrofoam cup. "Yeah, Sheriff. He was in earlier."

"Guess he'd be home, then, by now," Rhodes said.

"Don't know about that. Said he was goin' fishing this morning."

"At the lake or around here?"

"Round here. I think he's probably at that tank used to serve the Thurston Gin."

"Any fish in there?"

"Bass, mostly. Used to be some cats in there, but I haven't heard of anybody takin' one of them in years. Lots of little perch, too, but nobody cares 'bout them."

"Pretty good bass?" Rhodes was not merely making conversation. He had a real love of fishing for bass, but he seldom got the chance.

"Not bad. Old Bill took one out of there last week, ought to've gone three–four pounds."

There hadn't been a cotton gin in Thurston for forty years, but everyone still referred to the Thurston Gin Tank, a body of water about a tenth of a mile square (not round, as most stock tanks in the area), with a smaller connecting tank beside it.

Up north, they call them "ponds," Rhodes thought as he drove up. He remembered some kids from New Jersey who had visited his family while he was growing up. He had offered to take them fishing in a local tank. "In a *tank*?" they had asked, incredulous. "You can't fish in a *tank*!" Turned out they thought a tank was a big iron barrel. Well, the Gin Tank was hardly that.

The sides of it were dammed around with earth, ten feet higher than the surrounding pasture. Johnson grass, berry vines, milkweed, Bermuda grass, and who knew what else grew in profusion over the pasture and the dam. Willow trees that no one had planted had grown up all over the dam, looking for the water that they needed so desperately in the heat of the summer months. On one side of the dam, the east side, there was a break that was bridged by several rotting planks. Water flowed under the planks from one tank to the other.

The old gin property was not fenced. It covered several acres of land just off the main road, within sight of the stores and homes of Thurston. The family that owned the land had long since moved to the city, but they refused to sell the property. They held out fond hopes that one day oil or gas would be discovered in the Thurston area, not a very likely possibility to Rhodes's mind, so they kept the land and paid their taxes with regularity. In the meantime, they had no intention of putting out any money on upkeep; the land was unfenced, and anyone who wanted to fish in the tank was welcome to do so.

Rhodes drove up as near the dam as he could get and parked his cruiser, leaving behind him two lines of crushed grass and weeds. He couldn't see anyone on the dam, but there was the old gray Chevrolet that Tomkins had driven up to Barrett's store the other day parked not far from a big hackberry tree. Rhodes got out of the car and started up on the dam. Beggar lice stuck to his pants legs, and he was sure that chiggers were leaping from the Johnson grass by the thousands to bury their heads in his flesh. It made him itch just to think about it, but there was nothing he could do.

When he got to the top of the dam he looked around. Tomkins was on the other side of the tank, in a shady spot between two willow trees. There was a camp stool nearby, but Tomkins was standing up with a cane pole under his left arm. With his right hand he was putting a large shiner on a hook. As Rhodes watched, he tossed the shiner out into the tank. After it hit and sank, a red and white plastic cork bobbed on the surface of the water.

Rhodes was mindful of the fisherman's etiquette that required him to remain silent to avoid scaring the fish. Rhodes wasn't sure he believed that noise made any difference, but he walked as silently as he could around the dam to where Tomkins was. By the time he got there, Tomkins was seated on the folding stool and casting a spinner bait into the tank with a cheap black rod and Zebco 33 reel.

"How're they biting?" Rhodes asked, hunkering down by Tomkins.

"So-so," Tomkins wheezed in his asthmatic way. "Stringer's over there." He indicated a stick anchored in the mud.

Rhodes walked over to the stick and saw that a nylon line was tied to it. He pulled up the line. As it emerged from the slightly muddy brown water, he saw, and felt, the fish. There were three, the line running through their gills and mouths. Two were fairly small, but the third weighed about three pounds. The water rolled off their scales, making them shine in the rays of the sun that came through the willow branches.

"Nice mess of fish," Rhodes said, lowering them back into the water. "I wouldn't mind catching a few like that myself."

Tomkins reeled in his spinner bait, but he didn't make another cast. "I get the feelin' you didn't come out here just to talk about the fishin'," he wheezed.

"That's right, Bill, I didn't." Rhodes turned to face him. At the same time his eyes caught a brief glimpse of something shiny in a grove of trees about a hundred yards away, something that he barely glimpsed over Tomkins's head. It was easy to see the trees, because Tomkins was seated in a gap between the two willows, and their branches and leaves were quite thin. Rhodes dismissed the shine, not even sure that he had seen it.

"I hear you've been telling some folks that Jeanne Clinton had quite a few visitors at night while Elmer was out," Rhodes said. "Now, you mentioned Hod Barrett to me, and then you hushed. If there was ever anybody else, though, you'd better tell me now. I'd hate to think you were hiding evidence of a crime from me."

Tomkins laid down his rod and reel. "Just a minute, Sheriff," he said. "You just hold your horses. I might've had a good reason for not tellin' you who else was there."

Rhodes shook his head. "No such thing, Bill. There's no good reason for hiding something when murder's involved. I know you went by there, and Hod did. Now I want to know who else."

Tomkins spit in the tank, then rubbed his hand over his face. "All right, I'll tell you. But you'll see why I didn't at first. I knew you'd find out. See, one of the others that stopped by to see Jeanne was your election opponent, Ralph Claymore." He paused to take a deep, rough breath. "I just didn't see how it would do you or Mr. Claymore either one any good for me to bring that up."

"One of the others, Bill? One of them? It's beginning to sound like Jeanne was holding open house whenever Elmer cut out for work." Rhodes shifted his weight and leaned a little forward. "It might make a man wonder if somebody who was seeing her got just a little jealous, maybe. Maybe he could have gotten so upset that he decided to do something about it."

Tomkins jumped up from his camp stool, angry. Rhodes thought he looked a little like Walter Brennan taking on Richard Crenna in an episode of "The Real McCoys." "You got no call to say that, Sheriff! Jeanne was just a sweet, nice girl. Let me tell you who . . ."

He never got to tell who because a number of things

happened almost simultaneously. Rhodes, no matter how much he tried later, was never able to get the sequence exactly straight in his mind.

He saw the flash again in the grove of trees, that was for sure. He remembered a few willow leaves and maybe part of a branch falling, and he was pretty sure that he heard the two rifle shots. What he remembered most, though, was the way that Bill Tomkins's head just seemed to sort of come apart, and how Tomkins dropped like a rock, rolled a couple of times, and came to a stop in the water, with the red stain seeming quite brown as it widened around him.

8

RHODES WAS UP over the tank dam and running toward the grove of trees almost before his eyes had time to take in the details of Tomkins's death. He ran through the chest-high Johnson grass without a thought of either cuts or chiggers. He didn't break any land speed records, but when he arrived he could hear that someone else was still scrambling around in there.

Sounds in the woods can be deceptive, and Rhodes paused to listen. He wasn't sure just which direction to take, so he plunged straight in, drawing his .38 as he did so. A twig lashed across his open eye, and tears began to flow. "Damn," he said, stumbling a bit as his foot caught in a thorn-covered vine that grew along the ground. He put the pistol back in its holster and used his hands to help clear his way.

While the grove was not a forest in any sense of the word, it was nevertheless dense, a reminder of what all the country around Thurston must have been like at one time, before the cotton farmers moved in and cleared all the land. Or *most* of the land. Occasionally, someone would have more space than he needed, or someone would just happen to like a little woods. In such cases a stand of trees would remain, and even an acre or two of trees could seem like a forest when a man was trying to run through it.

Rhodes soon realized that he had little chance of catching up with anyone except by sheer accident, but he kept on. Sometimes he got lucky.

Unfortunately, this was not one of the times, and after fifteen minutes of blundering about, ripping his pants leg and getting an angry scratch across the back of his hand besides, Rhodes gave up and went back to the tank.

Tomkins still lay where he had fallen, and Rhodes felt a real surge of regret tinged with guilt. He hadn't for a minute really suspected that the scrawny Tomkins had killed Jeanne Clinton. He'd only been trying to stir him up and maybe get Tomkins to tell him something he could use. Instead, he'd gotten him killed. It was obvious that whoever had been hiding in the trees was waiting for a shot at Tomkins, who couldn't be seen over the top of the dam as long as he was sitting down. But when he'd jumped up, angry at Rhodes's insinuations, he'd become a target.

Even worse, in one way, was the fact that Tomkins had been just about to give Rhodes another name. He'd never do that now.

Rhodes pulled the body out of the water and into the shade of the willow tree, thinking of an old folk song that he'd heard The Weavers sing on the radio when he was young: "Bury Me Beneath the Willow." He felt sorry for Bill Tomkins, but there was nothing he could do for him now. He pulled the fish stringer out of the water, pulled the cord through their gills and mouths, and released them. Each one held itself motionless for a second or two, then twitched and was gone. Then he turned to go into town and make the necessary calls.

He used the telephone in Hod Barrett's store. Larry Bell was at the counter. "Sure, Sheriff, you're welcome to use the phone," he said. "I don't think old Hod would mind."

"Where's Hod?" Rhodes asked as he dialed.

"Don't know," Bell said. "He just asked me to take over for a while. I do it ever now and again when he needs to step out. He's been gone about an hour now, so I expect he'll be back pretty quick. What's up?"

"Never mind," Rhodes said, as the justice of the peace answered his ring.

* * *

74

It took the rest of the morning to get things straight at the crime scene, but Rhodes learned a little in the process. He found, eventually, two brass cartridge cases near a huge hackberry tree, and there was enough scuffing on the trunk to indicate that someone had recently climbed it. There was a broad limb where someone could have sat and had a good view of the gap between the willows at the Gin Tank.

The casings were for a .30-.30, but that didn't mean much. Probably every male in Thurston had a deer rifle, and probably every one of those rifles was a .30-.30. The casings were made by Remington, which was even less of a clue.

Rhodes questioned most of the residents of the nearby houses, but none of them had heard the shots or noticed anything out of the ordinary, like a man running along the road with a rifle in his hand, though to tell the truth such a sight was not so rare in Thurston as an outsider might think it to be.

So Rhodes drove back to Clearview with another corpse on his hands and too many more unanswered questions to count. He'd called Hack on the telephone, again avoiding the radio for whatever good that would do, so he didn't bother to go by the jail. He stopped for a quick hamburger, and then headed for Ralph Claymore's house.

Claymore was a gentleman rancher, and he was just as likely to be at home as not. Years ago, he had discovered the benefits of the U. S. Government's generous soil bank program and found that he could make more money *not* growing cotton than he could make by actually growing the stuff. He'd gradually begun buying up all the land he could and putting that in the soil bank along with what he'd already owned. Uncle Sam was making the payments, and Claymore was taking it easy instead of getting all hot and sweaty in the fields. After that, Claymore saw the advantages that were open to a thinking businessman. He traded in cattle and horses, and as often as not he came away the winner in any deal that he was involved in. As the years went by, he began to accumulate a sizeable bank account, to drive bigger and bigger cars, and to wear double-knit jeans instead of the old cotton overalls he'd started in.

Claymore's house was about a quarter mile outside of Clearview on a well-maintained county road. The commissioners always seemed to be able to get Claymore's road taken care of. The house, like Claymore himself, had an impressive appearance. It was long and low, made of adobe brick, with a red tile roof, probably the only tile roof in Clearview, Rhodes thought. The yard, though not up to the standards of Hod Barrett's wife, was neat enough. There was a long gooseneck trailer in the paved drive, with a Lincoln nearly as long parked beside it.

Rhodes wondered why anyone in his right mind would want to drive a county Plymouth when he could be driving his own Lincoln. He pulled in behind the trailer and parked the car.

Claymore's doorbell played "The Eyes of Texas." Or maybe it was "I've Been Workin' on the Railroad," but Rhodes wouldn't have bet on it. He wondered if the voters of Blacklin County knew about that doorbell, but somehow he doubted that it was a valid campaign issue.

The door was opened by Claymore's wife, who unfortunately looked more like his mother. She was one of those women who had gone gray with a vengeance and who was also small and rather frail. Add to that a dry skin that wrinkled early, and you got a woman who looked older than her years. She seldom appeared with Claymore at any of his campaign speeches. "Why, it's Sheriff Rhodes," she said.

"Hello, Mrs. Claymore," Rhodes said. "I'd like to speak to your husband if he's in."

"Of course," she said, opening the door all the way and stepping to the side. "Come right in. I'll call Ralph."

She proceeded to do exactly that in a voice much stronger than Rhodes would have expected. Her voice echoed in the entrance hall, and if Claymore was in the house he must have heard it. In fact, he appeared almost at once.

76

Ralph Claymore at home was just like Ralph Claymore anywhere else—except for the hat. He had on the western shirt, the boots, the belt with the big silver buckle, but no hat. His black, wavy hair was in stark contrast to his wife's sullen gray.

If Claymore was surprised to see Dan Rhodes in his hall, he didn't show it. He stuck out his right hand and grabbed Rhodes's hand, pumping it as if Rhodes were one of his favorite constituents. "Dan, Dan, good to see you," he said heartily. "Come on in. Dora can make us some coffee."

"No coffee, thanks," Rhodes said to Mrs. Claymore. "I just need to talk to Ralph here about the campaign."

"Of course, of course," Claymore said. "Come on down to my study. We can talk there. Dora's not really very interested in my electioneering, are you, honey?"

Dora shook her gray head, and Claymore began steering Rhodes away. "You just go on in the den and watch a little TV, honey," he said. "I think it's about time for "Family Feud " now, and you know how you hate to miss that one. Mr. Rhodes and I won't be long."

Dora obediently wandered off in the direction of what Rhodes assumed to be the den, and Claymore guided him down the hall to the study.

When they stepped through the door, Rhodes wondered just what it was that Claymore studied. There was a huge oak desk with a glass top, and behind it was a wall covered with a built-in bookshelf that ran the length of the room, a good twelve feet. But there were relatively few books on the shelves. It looked to Rhodes as if Claymore owned the complete works of Louis L'Amour, and very little else in the realm of literature. The rest of the shelf space was taken up by western bric-a-brac—rusty spurs, lengths of maybe fifty different kinds of barbed wire mounted on boards, mounted pistols, stirrups, rifles (some new, some old, and at least one .30-.30), and even an old hat or two.

Rhodes turned and looked around the room. On the other

walls there were several framed pictures, all of them on western themes. None of the pictures was a Remington, but there was at least one that was a pretty good imitation. There were what looked like Indian rugs on the hardwood flooring.

Claymore went behind the desk and sat in his brown leather executive chair. "Make yourself comfortable," he said to Rhodes. "Have a seat." He gestured to a hard-bottomed wooden chair that sat near the desk.

Rhodes hadn't been tricked into the teacher/student relationship in years. "I'll stand, I think," he said. "There are a couple of questions I'd like to ask you."

Claymore leaned back and laced his fingers behind his neck. "Ask away, but before you get started, let me tell you that what happened the other night in Milsby had nothing to do with me. I don't work that way. I'm trying to run as clean a campaign as I can, and I wouldn't stoop to mud-slinging of any sort, as I'm sure you wouldn't." Though Claymore's voice was as deep and convincing as ever, Rhodes thought he detected a slight quaver in it.

"I'm sure that you'd never have looked up that Wayne character on your own," Rhodes said. "Of course, I'm having it checked into. But that's not my question."

Despite his efforts to appear relaxed, Claymore was definitely showing signs of discomfort. Although he must have had his air conditioner set at around sixty-eight degrees, there was a faint sheen of sweat on his upper lip. "I see," he said. "Just what did you want to talk about then?"

Rhodes stepped back from the desk a few paces and leaned on the doorframe. "I suppose that what I have to ask could have some bearing on the kind of campaign I run," he said. "It has to do with Jeanne Clinton."

Claymore came forward in his chair and placed his palms down on the glass top of the desk. There was nothing else at all on the desk, not even a picture or an ashtray. "Yes, that was an unfortunate incident," he said. "Very unfortunate. You have my word that I won't mention it while the campaign is on. I realize that no enforcement, even the strictest, can prevent every crime, especially a crime of passion."

"Did I mention passion?" Rhodes asked. "Besides, that's not what I meant at all."

Claymore turned his palms up and looked into them as if trying to read his lifeline. "What did you mean, then?"

Rhodes straightened. "I think you know. I think you'd better tell me, though, instead of having me tell you. Otherwise, I might somehow get the impression that you have some pressing reason for avoiding the mention of the Clinton murder in your campaign, some reason that doesn't have a damn thing to do with clean politics. Or dirty ones either."

Claymore shook his head without looking up. "Would you mind shutting the door, Rhodes?"

Rhodes stepped into the hall and pulled the door shut. "Let's have it," he said.

Claymore met Rhodes's eyes. "It's hard to explain," he said.

"I can imagine," Rhodes responded. "But don't worry. If you're not involved in the murder, you can trust me to keep quiet about your involvement. I don't want to win an election by throwing mud any more than you do."

"All right," Claymore said with a sigh. "I guess it's really simple enough. I own some property in Thurston, so I go over there pretty often. Sometimes I stop by at Hod Barrett's store for a Coke and to talk to the fellas there. One day I met Jeanne in there, and one thing just led to another." He raised his hands and then let them fall limply. "You've seen Dora. It's not just how she looks. It's how she lives, her whole attitude. She never wants to go anywhere or do anything. She just sits around the house all day watching that damn TV. Game shows. My God, if I never see or hear another game show as long as I live, it'll be all right with me. 'Wheel of Fortune,' twice a day. 'Family Feud.' Even reruns of 'Let's Make a Deal.' She won't even let me talk to her when they're on!"

"Sounds bad all right," Rhodes said. He meant it. He hated

game shows. He watched only comedy reruns and old movies.

"Anyway," Claymore said, "Jeanne was easy to talk to. She liked people, and she had a sense of humor. I'd forgotten what it was like to laugh with a woman. So I started dropping by to see her when her husband wasn't around. Not that there was anything wrong in what we did, you understand. Not a thing! But I just felt that her husband might not understand."

You and three or four others, Rhodes thought. That Jeanne Clinton should have been charging by the hour, like a psychiatrist. She could have gotten rich.

"You ever see anyone else over there?" Rhodes asked.

"No, no one. I was always very care . . . very *discreet*."

"You were seen, of course," Rhodes said. "You should have known that in a town the size of Thurston everyone knows everything that goes on."

"Elmer?" said Claymore. "Is he the one . . . ?"

"Not Elmer. Bill Tomkins."

"Tomkins? I think I've met him at Barrett's store. Is he the one with the breathing problem?"

"It won't be bothering him anymore," Rhodes said. "Someone shot him with a .30-.30 this morning."

Claymore came apart after that. He offered to go get Dora to tell Rhodes that she and Claymore had been in the house all morning, offered to let him take in his .30-.30 to see if the firing pin matched the print of the one on the casings, begged Rhodes not to release the information that Claymore had been seeing Jeanne.

"I told you not to worry," Rhodes said when Claymore ran down. "But you know I have to investigate this aspect of the murder. If you had anything to do with it, anything at all, God help you."

"I didn't," Claymore said. "I swear it. I'll pull out of the election campaign if you want me to."

"I said I didn't want to win that way, and I meant it," Rhodes said. "You can continue your campagin exactly as you have."

80

Claymore's eyes reflected his gratitude. "I never said you weren't a good sheriff," he said. "About this Terry Wayne . . ."

"I don't think I want to hear it," Rhodes said. "I'll deal with him myself. It's a matter for the department. If there's anything to his accusations, I'll find out. I'd just as soon not have any private citizens mixing in, if it's all the same to you."

"I understand," Claymore said, rising from his chair. "I'd like to shake your hand, Sheriff." He extended his right hand.

Rhodes took it. Maybe he'll vote for me, he thought. But somehow he doubted it.

The blast of hot air that escaped from Rhodes's car when he opened the door almost bowled him over. It seemed especially bad after the cool comfort of Claymore's air-conditioned house. He steeled himself, but the touch of the vinyl seats caused him to shift about briskly nevertheless. Sticking the key into the ignition slot on the steering column was like touching the glowing tip of a welding rod.

Rhodes started the car and turned the air conditioner on high. Hot air from the vents hit him in the face, but he drove around until the temperature was bearable. While he drove, he thought about what had just gone on. Just how badly did he want to win the election? How much did it really mean to him? Had he really meant what he said to Claymore? And how sure could he be that Claymore was telling him the truth?

The last thought led to an interesting complication. What if Claymore and Jeanne were actually quite involved? What if Jeanne had threatened to let their involvement be known? The question then became one of how badly Claymore wanted to win. Would he have killed to prevent Jeanne from spoiling his chances? Would he have killed Tomkins to keep Tomkins from talking?

Rhodes didn't think so, and he was a man who trusted his hunches. Nevertheless, it wouldn't hurt to do a little checking on Claymore's whereabouts on the night Jeanne Clinton had died.

9

RHODES DROVE OUT to Sally's Truck Stop. He hadn't asked anyone else to check on Elmer's story about eating breakfast there the morning of Jeanne's death, and it was time somebody did so.

Sally's was a small wooden frame building set nearly a block back off the highway. The block was taken up with a wide white-gravel parking lot, so white that it hurt Rhodes's eyes in the glare of the sun. He knew that the lot was spotted with oil stains from the big trucks that stopped there, but he couldn't see them from the road.

At this time of the day, Sally's was quiet. There was only one eighteen wheeler parked in the lot, right up near the door. Rhodes drove his car over the uneven graveled surface, parked beside the truck, and got out.

The inside of Sally's was cool and spotlessly clean, though maybe not as clean as Hod Barrett's wife kept her house. There was a long formica counter with stools, and a row of booths covered in red vinyl. The trucker was sitting on one of the stools drinking a cup of coffee and eating a piece of Sally's justly renowned pecan pie.

Leaving a stool between himself and the trucker, Rhodes sat down. Sally came out of the kitchen. She was a bottle blond of indeterminate age, though Rhodes had been around long enough in the same town to make a pretty accurate guess. He pegged her at fifty-five. She looked as if she enjoyed her own pecan pies.

"Afternoon, Sheriff," she said. She had a deep voice, almost as deep as a man's. "A Dr Pepper, right?"

"Right," Rhodes said. He loved Dr Peppers and had drunk a lot of them in Sally's.

She brought him the drink and he sipped it while the trucker finished his pie, paid up, and left. When Sally came back down to his part of the counter, they talked about the weather, about her business, and about her customers, not all of whom were as taciturn as the trucker who had just left.

When the opportunity came, Rhodes asked about Elmer Clinton. "He come in here often?"

"Often enough," Sally said. "Course he ain't been in since his wife got killed. He liked to come in for a little breakfast, shoot the breeze a little. He was in here the very morning y'all found her body, as a matter of fact. Lordy, that must've been a shock to him. He really loved that girl. Poor fella."

"Poor fella?" Rhodes said.

"Yeah. I mean, you take a guy like him, he was lucky to get him a wife at all, much less one like Jeanne, young and pretty like she was. Course she was a little wild for a while there, but she settled down and made Elmer a fine wife. Why, he practically worshipped the ground that girl walked on. Many's the morning he'd sit here and tell everybody what a lucky man he was. Lots of the fellas that come in here, well, they don't always talk so nice about their wives, but not Elmer. I surely do feel sorry for that man."

Rhodes thanked her for his drink and paid her thirty-five cents. Then he went out into the heat again, but not to his car. There was a public phone at the side of Sally's, and he went over and dropped a quarter in the slot, then dialed Claymore's number.

Mrs. Claymore answered. Rhodes could hear the frantic voice of an emcee in the background. He identified himself and then asked to speak to her husband.

"Why, I believe he's out doing a little campaigning, Sheriff," she said. "Can I have him call you when he gets back?"

Rhodes was glad to hear the news that Claymore wasn't home. "No," he said, "no need to bother him. I just wanted to ask him about that little rally the Clearview Breakfast Club sponsored last Tuesday night. I didn't get to attend, and I thought I'd see if your husband could tell me about it. I meant to ask earlier, but it slipped my mind."

"Oh dear," said Mrs. Claymore. "I'm sure he couldn't help you. Ralph and I never miss "The A-Team" on Tuesday nights."

"Well, thanks anyway, Mrs. Claymore," Rhodes said, hanging up the phone. Claymore wasn't necessarily in the clear, but he'd been home the early part of Tuesday night.

Rhodes got in his car, called up Buddy on the radio, and asked him to meet him at Ferguson's Feed Store.

Claude Ferguson was a cousin of Claire's, and he and Rhodes had been friends for years. He didn't mind at all if the sheriff used the back of his feed store for a meeting place if he wanted to discuss something that he didn't want to talk about at the jail. There was a small parking lot behind the store that no one ever used, and any conversations held in the rear part of the cavernous building were easily kept private.

Rhodes liked the place. It was an old tin building, with its wooden floor set up on concrete blocks. In many places the tin sides were gapped, and there were double-wide doors on all sides, all of which contributed to the free circulation of air. There was a wall between the small front section of the store and the back area so that the front could be heated and cooled. The wall had a large door in it, but the door was always closed unless someone was loading feed through it.

Rhodes pulled into the parking lot, got out, and stepped through the back door. He was greeted with the distinctive smell of feed stores everywhere, a combination of ground corn, wheat shorts, horse and mule feed mixed with molasses, laying mash, pig starter, and who knew what else. There was a strong ammonium tinge from the fertilizer, and just a whiff of Diazanon as well. It was a smell that Rhodes didn't mind at all.

He walked between rows of paper and burlap feed sacks stacked as high as his head, and even higher. When he came to a stack of shelled corn that was about waist high, he sat on the top sack to wait for Buddy.

Buddy wasn't long in appearing. He came in and sat across from Rhodes on a red, white, and blue sack of hen scratch.

Buddy didn't look much like a deputy sheriff. Rhodes had never quite been able to decide just exactly what Buddy *did* look like. He was tall and thin, and he could never get a uniform shirt (or any other shirt) that quite fit. The sleeves were always too short, or if they were long enough, the shoulder seams hung over his shoulders. His head didn't match his body. It was far too big for his thin neck, and it always seemed in a precarious state of balance.

His appearance didn't affect his work, however. Buddy was good at his job.

"Had any time to look into that Terry Wayne business?" Rhodes asked when Buddy had settled himself.

"Sure have, Sheriff," Buddy said. His voice was a nasal tenor. "I talked to the man himself."

"And?"

"And I think you better talk to him, Sheriff," Buddy said seriously, his big head bobbing up and down. "I b'lieve that old boy really thinks he has a case."

Rhodes sighed and leaned back against the stack of corn sacks at his back. "You don't think he's bluffing?"

"I didn't say what I thought. I said what he thinks. If you get what I mean." Buddy pulled up a thin knee and locked his hands around it.

"I'm not sure that I do," Rhodes said. "Does he have a case, or doesn't he?"

"I don't know," Buddy said stubbornly. "I just know he *thinks* he has a case. He's getting himself a lawyer and everything."

Rhodes groaned. "What about that business with Claymore?"

"Well, I think you could say that it was mostly Wayne's idea."

"It's that 'mostly' part that I'm interested in," Rhodes said.

"You don't have to be diplomatic about it." Rhodes suspected that Buddy was watching his words because if Claymore were elected and Rhodes were out of a job, Buddy would still be a deputy. The county wasn't exactly on the spoils system.

"What I mean is, I think he went to Claymore with the idea. It wasn't something that Claymore knew about in advance. I could tell that much. If the fight was staged, Claymore didn't know a thing about it, but I guess he didn't mind using it."

Rhodes had just about reached the same conclusion after his talk with Claymore, and it didn't make him happy. "OK, Buddy, thanks. You can get back on your run," he said.

But Buddy didn't get up. It was plain that he had something more to say, but that he wasn't quite sure how to say it. Finally he got it out. "Sheriff, how much do you know about Johnny Sherman?" Instead of waiting for an answer, he rushed on. "I mean, I know he goes out with your daughter and all, and you wouldn't of hired him if he hadn't been a good man for the job, but this Wayne fella really seems to think he can get the department on this. I mean, he's convinced that he and his pal were whipped up on by Johnny for no reason at all."

Despite the sinking feeling in his stomach, Rhodes tried to be optimistic. "Look at it this way, Buddy. Nobody we ever arrested was guilty of a thing to hear him tell it, was he. Can you ever remember arresting a guilty party in your whole carrer?"

"No, Sheriff, not when you put it like that. But this Wayne ain't like that. He sounds mighty damn truthful to me. I'm afraid that with a good lawyer, he can really cause some trouble."

"Well, we'll just have to wait and see about that," Rhodes said. "You can be sure of one thing. If Johnny did anything wrong, I'll find out about it." He stood up, clapped Buddy on the shoulder, and walked out to his car.

When he got back to the jail, Rhodes let Hack catch him up

on the latest happenings. "That Polish fella's wife came and got him this morning," Hack said.

"His wife?" Rhodes said. "And I thought you said he wasn't Polish."

"Wasn't," Hack said. "He was just as American as you and me."

"Then why was he speaking Polish?" Rhodes felt vaguely that he was playing his part in one of Hack's Abbott and Costello routines.

"Wasn't. Told you that already. He was drunk, but he was trying to make us think he was Polish, so he was just gabblin' away."

Rhodes hated to ask why, but he knew it was expected, so he did.

"Because he was trying to get away from his wife. I think he hoped we might ship him to Poland or something," Hack said. Then he laughed. "After a look at that wife of his, I didn't blame him. Things might not be too good in Poland, but that fella had a lot to contend with at home. I guess any place'd be better, to him."

Rhodes grinned. At least there was one less problem for him to deal with. "Billy Joe started talking yet?" he asked.

"Not yet," Hack said. "I think he misses the Polish fella."

Rhodes went out and up to the cells. Billy Joe didn't appear too happy to see him, but at least he didn't cower and babble. He just sat quietly on his bunk and looked at Rhodes. Lawton wasn't around, so Rhodes walked over and rattled the door of Billy Joe's cell. It was safely locked.

"I'd give a lot to know how you got out of that cell, Billy Joe," Rhodes said. He waited for a minute, but there was no answer. Billy Joe continued to sit quietly, hardly seeming to breathe.

"Give a lot to know just what happened over in Thurston the other night, too," Rhodes went on. "Seems like you'd have a mighty interesting story to tell."

Billy Joe still said nothing.

"That blood, now, that blood on your shirt surely makes things look bad for you," Rhodes said. "It wasn't your blood, Billy Joe. It looks to me like it was Jeanne Clinton's blood, and she's sure enough dead. I don't guess word's got out in town yet that we've got you here, or there might be a lot of folks wanting to know if you were the guilty party. They could cause a lot of trouble, Billy Joe."

Billy Joe looked vaguely troubled, and Rhodes wondered just how much of what he'd said had been understood. Billy Joe might not be the most intelligent man in Clearview, but he wasn't an idiot. He must have had some idea of the trouble he was in, and Rhodes was convinced that he could tell a lot about Jeanne's murder if he would just open up. But Rhodes was running out of time. People in Clearview were generally a tolerant lot, but the killing of Bill Tomkins was going to get the whole county in an uproar, and Rhodes was going to be pressed to come up with some answers. Billy Joe was going to have to talk, or else Rhodes was going to have to find the answers elsewhere.

Rhodes didn't want to pressure Billy Joe. There was a delicate balance in Billy Joe's head that he didn't want to disturb because he still believed Billy Joe to be incapable of murder. He decided to give it one more try, but a quiet one.

"I think you know I've always treated you right, Billy Joe. No one here's ever hurt you, and we won't hurt you this time. Just let me know if you want to talk. I'll listen, and we can get this mess all straightened out."

Billy Joe looked thoughtful. Finally, he spoke. "Smokes?" he asked. He pulled out a battered package of Merits from somewhere inside his shirt.

"I'm surprised you have any of those left," Rhodes said. "I'll send Hack up with a light in a minute. Anything else you want to talk about?"

Billy Joe shook his head.

"All right," Rhodes said. "But pretty soon we've got to get

this discussed." He left the block and went back down to talk to Hack Jensen.

"Billy Joe wants a light. Has he been smoking much?"

"All the damn time," Hack said. "He must have cigarettes stashed all in those clothes of his."

"Well, go up in a minute and give him a light. Anything else to report for today, or has it been a quiet Friday for a change?"

"Now you know better than that, Sheriff," Hack said, "but nothing of a major nature. I guess the biggest thing's some fella named Adkins who wants to report his car stolen."

" 'Wants to'? Why can't he just report it?" Rhodes asked, suspecting that he was setting himself up again.

"Can't exactly call it stolen, I guess," Hack said. "He knows where it is, and all."

It was too late for Rhodes to back out now, so he went on. "If he knows where it is, why doesn't he just get it?"

"Can't get it. He can *see* it, but he can't exactly get it. I mean, he *could* get it, but then he might be doing something illegal himself. I need you to interpret the law on this one for me."

Rhodes managed to resist the impulse to ask Hack to get to the point, but it wasn't easy. "If you'll explain it, I'll be glad to interpret for you," he said.

"You remember that drunk we had two weeks back, drove his car into old man Carlen's field off one of the county roads?" Hack asked.

Rhodes said that he remembered.

"Well, that drunk was Adkins," Hack said. "Took him about two days in the block to sleep it off, as I recall it."

"I'm sure that's right," Rhodes said. Hack usually kept up with the prisoners with great accuracy. He could go back in his memory a year or more without error.

"Well, by the time he got on his feet and out of jail, he didn't have enough money to get that car towed in. It'd been raining about then, and that car was stuck pretty good. That ground out there's black and sticky as it can be. No way he could just drive it out."

"But he's got the money now?" Rhodes asked.

"Yeah, he's got it now."

"Then what's the problem?" Rhodes was near exasperation.

"Problem is, now old man Carlen's gone and repaired the fence where Adkins smashed through it. Brand-new bob wire fence, stretched tight as a young gal's pants. Get that car out, you're going to have to cut that fence. And old man Carlen wouldn't take very well to somebody cutting his brand-new fence."

Rhodes knew Carlen, and he knew the old man had a salty temper. "I expect Mr. Carlen built that fence out of spite," he told Hack.

"I expect you're right about that," Hack said. "But a fence is a fence, any way you look at it."

"I'm going to lose a vote any way I go about this one," Rhodes said.

Hack looked at him disdainfully. "You oughtn't joke about a thing like that, Sheriff," he said. "You know a vote don't mean a thing to you where it's a question of right or wrong."

"Thanks, Hack. I wish everyone in the county thought that way. But you're right. Something's got to be done, and no matter what Mr. Carlen thinks, Adkins has a right to his car."

"I'll call him myself," Hack said.

"All right, but use my name if you have to. Tell him I'll bring my own wire cutters out there if he wants to make it official."

"I don't think we'll have to worry about that," Hack said. "I think he just wanted to make a stir, and now that he's done it he'll probably calm down."

"It's getting a little late in the day," Rhodes said. "Save it till tomorrow why don't you. It'll make a good way to start the day."

90

"Yeah, if something else don't happen by then," Hack said. "Don't try to cheer me up," Rhodes told him. "I'm going home for supper. Then tonight I'll be going back to Thurston for a little talk with Elmer Clinton. Don't call me unless it's an emergency."

Hack looked hurt. "Have I ever called you when it wasn't?"

"Guess not," Rhodes said as he went out the door.

Rhodes was eating a bologna sandwich when Kathy came into the kitchen and joined him. "I wish you'd let me fix you a decent meal," she said. Rhodes looked ruefully at the limp sandwich. "Someday I will," he said. "I'm on the jump now, what with that latest killing."

"I heard about it on the news," Kathy said. Clearview, though small, had both an AM and an FM radio station. The FM station, trying to cut into the listenership of the older, more established AM one, did a lot of local news-talk shows.

"Any commentary?" Rhodes asked.

"Just a straight report. Not even any mention of a crime wave right here in Blacklin County," Kathy said.

"Not exactly a crime wave," Rhodes said. "But I guess for a town of Thurston's size it looks like one." He paused. "Speaking of Thurston, how's Johnny?"

Kathy looked down at the top of the round oak table. "Fine, I guess."

"You guess? What's the matter? Trouble between you two?"

"Not trouble, exactly. It . . . well, it's hard to explain."

Rhodes laid his sandwich, or what was left of it, down on his napkin. He never bothered with a plate when he ate alone. "Want to try? Explaining, I mean."

"I don't know," Kathy said. "He's been . . . different the last few days. Maybe that business about the lawsuit has bothered him. I don't know. He doesn't want to talk about it. He just gets upset if I mention it."

"He get that way often?" Rhodes picked up his sandwich. After what Buddy had told him, he didn't like the way this was sounding.

"Not often. He's moody, though, and sometimes a little pushy. As I said, it's hard to explain."

Rhodes stuffed the last of the sandwich in his mouth. "You still going to be seeing him?"

"Oh, I suppose so. He'll get over it, whatever it is."

"Do you ever think maybe it's time for you to get out of Clearview, maybe get a teaching job somewhere that has more to offer a young woman like you?" Rhodes smiled. "Not that I haven't liked your being here, but I can take care of myself now."

Kathy looked up at him and grinned. "Or maybe you've found someone else who can take care of you now," she said.

Rhodes was surprised to find himself nearly blushing, not so much because he was embarrassed as that his daughter could read him so well. "You mean Ivy Daniels, I guess," he said.

"Yes," she said, "and I think it's just fine."

"We've just been out the one time, and that was business," Rhodes said, aware that he was being a bit deceitful.

"And that's all there is to it?"

"Well, not exactly. We've made sort of a date to go out tomorrow night," Rhodes said. He felt like a schoolboy.

Kathy's grin turned into a smile. "I'm not sure that I'm ready to leave Clearview and Johnny just yet," she said, "but when I go you'll be in good hands." She pushed away from the table and stood up. "Have a good night, Dad."

Rhodes watched her walk away, not having much to say. He thought for a minute of Claire, but the memory did not jab him with a sharp pain under his heart as it would have only days before. If Kathy approved of Ivy Daniels, then his own feelings couldn't be too far out of line. He just hoped he wasn't reading too much into one date and the prospect of another.

Rhodes got up from the table and wiped the bread crumbs

into his hand with the napkin. Then he dusted the crumbs into the trash basket and tossed the napkin in after them. There was one advantage to eating alone. The clean-up was easy. He still had plenty of time to drive over to Thurston and talk to Elmer Clinton.

10

IT WAS ONLY seven o'clock when Rhodes got on the road, still plenty of daylight left. To the west, in the far distance, he could see a huge bank of black clouds building up. Ninety-five percent of the rainstorms came in from the west, and this looked to be a pretty good one. It was still a while off, though. In a minute the sun would sink behind the cloud bank and the evening would get cool and gray. It was the kind of weather Rhodes liked, and besides, if it rained, maybe some of Claymore's cardboard signs would get drenched and fall apart. At the very least they would get awfully wrinkled when the sun dried them out the next day.

He drove up to Elmer's house and parked in front. Elmer's car was parked by the chinaberry tree as usual. A couple of branches from the tree actually extended out over the car, and Rhodes saw a couple of chickens gone to roost in them. That wouldn't be much good for the finish on Elmer's car, Rhodes thought.

Yellow light spilled out of the screen door. Rhodes stepped up on the porch and knocked. Elmer walked into view. "Come in," he said.

Elmer and the room were both changed since Rhodes's last visit. The room had been thoroughly cleaned, the floors scrubbed, all the magazines and beer cans picked up. In fact, the room was immaculate. Rhodes found himself wondering for a second if Mrs. Barrett had been there.

Elmer reached out and shook the sheriff's hand. "Have a seat," he said. His voice and eyes were clear and steady. It was evident that he'd stopped drinking quite a while ago. His thinning hair was carefully combed.

Rhodes sat in a wooden rocker and glanced around the room. Nothing had been changed, except that there was now an eight-by-ten color picture of Jeanne in a gold frame atop the TV set.

"You found the man who killed my Jeanne yet, Sheriff?" Clinton asked.

"No, not yet, Elmer. I think it's time you gave me a little more help, though," Rhodes said, making himself comfortable.

"What's that supposed to mean?" Clinton asked. He continued to stand, massaging his thick left arm with his right hand.

"It's supposed to mean that the last time I talked to you, I didn't want to take advantage of your grief," Rhodes said. "But I think you lied to me, and I don't like being lied to when I'm investigating a crime. Lying makes a fella look guilty, sometimes."

Clinton drew himself up to his full five feet six with a deep breath. Rhodes pretended not to notice.

"I mean it, Elmer," he said. "You went on and on about how there was just no chance that Jeanne had been seeing anybody while you were off at work. Well, she had. In fact, it begins to look like she'd been seeing about half the damn town, along with a few folks from Clearview. And don't tell me you didn't know it."

"That goddamn Bill Tomkins!" Clinton spat the sentence out along with the breath he'd been holding. "That sonuvabitch had a poison tongue. I know what he was saying, all right, but it was all lies! My Jeanne was an angel on earth! That girl was as pure as the snow!"

Elmer's face was getting as red as a rooster's comb. Rhodes hoped he didn't have heart disease. He didn't say anything for a minute, then looked at Elmer's thinning hair. "How much older than Jeanne were you, Elmer?" he asked.

"God*damn* it, Sheriff! God*damn* it! What right you got to talk like that? What right you got to say those things?" Clinton waved his arms around, then sank to the couch.

"I didn't say anything, Elmer," Rhodes said mildly. "I just asked a simple question. Seems to me there'd be no harm in answering."

"You know it anyway, goddamn you."

"No, I don't know it, but I can make a pretty good guess," Rhodes said. "I'd guess nearly thirty years."

"Close enough," Clinton said. "Close enough. And now you're wondering what'd make a girl that young, 'specially one that looked as good as Jeanne, marry an old goat like me."

"I might have wondered about that," Rhodes said.

"Well, I'll tell you. She liked me." Clinton shook his head. "It was as simple as that. I know it's hard to believe, but it's the truth. She'd been married once before, you know. Her husband got killed in some kind of accident up there on that Alaska pipeline, and she was livin' by herself. We met a time or two and got to talkin', you know. Lord, that girl loved to talk. Anyway, one thing led to another and we just got married. Never had an argument or a fight, and that's a fact. She was the best girl in the world."

Rhodes was afraid that Clinton might get maudlin again, so he changed the subject back to what Elmer was trying to avoid. "She liked to talk, all right. She liked to talk so much that when you went off to work she talked to anybody that came around."

Clinton sprang off the couch. "Don't say that, Sheriff. Don't ever say that."

"It's true, Elmer, and you might as well face it. Bill Tomkins might have been a gossip, but he wasn't a liar. I can give you the names of three men, including him, who dropped by on your wife. And I think you knew all about it." Rhodes stood up.

Elmer Clinton shook his head. "You're wrong, Sheriff. I

didn't know. I never even dreamed it." His shoulders sagged. "I never even dreamed it," he said again.

Looking at him there, Rhodes believed him. "I'm sorry, then, Elmer, but it's true. I've been told by people who'd be better off if they hadn't been here. They weren't lying."

Elmer Clinton just stood there, shaking his head. Rhodes let himself out the screen door and walked to his car. He could hear the thunder in the distance now, and he saw a faint streak of lightning behind a cloud. There was a tang of ozone in the air. He got in the Plymouth and drove away.

It was raining lightly by the time Rhodes got back to Clearview, and he stopped by the jail to check in. Hack and Lawton were sitting around talking as he came in the door.

"Thought you was going over to Thurston, Sheriff," Hack said.

"I'm back," Rhodes said. "Anything come up tonight?"

"Just the usual round of drunks and wrecks," Hack said. "Nothing special. It'll get worse, though, what with this rain."

That was the one aspect of rain that Rhodes disliked. It slicked the highways and always increased the number of accidents. It was particularly bad on weekends. "Highway patrol will have its hands full, all right," he said. "How's Billy Joe?"

"Still nothing to say," Lawton said. "I check that door real good now, every time I go by."

"Don't worry about it," Rhodes said. "What's been bothering me is how he got through this room without anybody seeing him."

Lawton and Hack looked at one another. They hadn't thought of that, just as Rhodes hadn't until driving back from Thurston. It was easy enough to imagine Billy Joe trying the door of his cell and finding it open, but it wasn't easy to imagine him getting down from the block and out past Hack. It must have happened, but Rhodes couldn't see how. He excused himself from not having thought of it earlier by recalling that he'd just gotten back from the candidates' forum. Seeing Mrs. Wilkie and being confronted by Terry Wayne all in the same night would be enough to play havoc with anybody's thought processes.

"Think about it," Rhodes said. "One or both of you had to be in here, unless you'd both stepped into the back room, and I know you wouldn't stay there for very long. Did anything unusual happen that you can remember?"

The two old men were silent, thinking back to the previous evening. "Seems like things went about as usual," Lawton said. "I recall Johnny coming in, and we did a little hoorawin' like we always do, but nothing out of the ordinary."

"No calls came in, I remember that," Hack added.

Then Lawton snapped his fingers. "We *was* both in that back room," he said. "Remember, Hack."

Hack obviously remembered. He shook his head ruefully. "Couple of dirty old men," he said.

"What do you mean?" Rhodes asked.

"Well," Hack said, "Johnny came in and checked the prisoners over, and when he came back down he said he had a copy of one of them men's magazines, one with some pretty good pictures of some movie star."

"Wasn't just some movie star," Lawton said. "It was that woman in one of them nighttime soaps. Fifty years old, she is, and looks just like a young girl. Hard to believe anybody nearly old enough for me or Hack here could look that good. 'Course she'd never give one of us a second look, I guess."

"That's the truth," Hack said, "but that's what it was, Sheriff. We couldn't of been out of here more than ten minutes, though."

"Didn't want one of the registered voters to come in and catch us lookin' at dirty pictures," Lawton said apologetically. "Goes to show where that kind of thing gets you, though. That must be when Billy Joe got by us."

"Hard to believe he's that smart," Rhodes said. He didn't

98

blame the two men for going to look at the magazine. He'd have been tempted himself.

"Maybe he's smarter than we give him credit for," Hack said. "Maybe he *did* kill Jeanne Clinton."

"Maybe," Rhodes said. "But I don't really believe it."

"Me neither," Hack said. "It was just a thought."

"And if he didn't, who did?" Lawton put in.

"I wish I could tell you," Rhodes said. "I really wish I could."

Rhodes reached home during a lull in the thunderstorm, which by then had become what the locals referred to as a real toad strangler. He managed to get from his car to the house with only minor water spotting.

Kathy was in her room, reading probably. Rhodes got ready for bed and turned on his television set in time to catch the last few minutes of *Hangman's Knot,* a western with Randolph Scott. Rhodes had always thought that Scott was a fine actor who had never received the recognition he was due. Could anybody name an actor who had consistently done such good work in as many low-budget westerns? Rhodes doubted it. He hoped that Donna Reed appreciated what kind of man she was getting at the picture's end. He had read somewhere that Scott was still alive and, incredibly, in California, and he hoped that was true. Scott deserved it.

Rhodes lay on his extra firm mattress and tried to drift off to sleep, but it was impossible. Too many things kept running through his mind. Usually he could go to sleep almost as soon as he lay down, but the murders of Jeanne Clinton and Bill Tomkins had really disturbed him. He kept thinking that he should know more than he did, that he was asking the wrong questions or the wrong people.

He thought about Jeanne. Barrett, Tomkins, and Claymore had all told him the same thing about her—that she was a wonderful girl who just liked to talk, that she was only someone who listened to them. Since only Tomkins seemed to know about the others, they obviously hadn't gotten together to prepare a story. Maybe they were telling the truth. That made Jeanne Clinton a really rare individual, but it didn't give anyone a motive to kill her, unless it was her husband.

But Elmer Clinton seemed genuinely grief-stricken over Jeanne's death. It was almost impossible for Rhodes to believe that Elmer had killed her. He was so incredibly protective of her reputation that he almost certainly would *not* have killed her, if only to keep her friendships with other men secret. He would have known that the secret would come out in any murder investigation.

Besides, it seemed to Rhodes that Jeanne's visitors were truly a secret from Elmer, who was shocked and angry about Bill Tomkins's gossip. He'd heard it, but he apparently hadn't believed it.

Of course, there was the possibility that one of the men had pressed Jeanne to do more than talk. Barrett certainly had the strength to beat her, for example.

But then, who killed Tomkins? Barrett hadn't been in his store when Rhodes arrived to call in the word of Tomkins's death. Where had he been?

And who was the other man that Tomkins had been about to mention when he'd been shot? A few more seconds, and Rhodes would have had himself another suspect, one whose name he couldn't even guess right now, unless he included Billy Joe, and he still wasn't ready for that.

Then there was Mrs. Barrett. She was a hardworking woman, no doubt tough as wet leather, but Rhodes couldn't picture her as the type to beat another woman. That seemed to him a man's crime, and if that made him a male chauvinist pig, then so be it. He'd just have to suffer the consequences. Even at that, he couldn't just exclude Mrs. Barrett entirely from his suspects.

When Rhodes finally drifted off to sleep, he dreamed that he was Randolph Scott and that Ivy Daniels was Donna Reed, or maybe it was Jeanne Clinton who was Donna, and Lee

Marvin was beating her, and Rhodes was trying to get to him to make him stop, and when he grabbed Marvin's arm, it wasn't Marvin who looked back at him but someone else, but Rhodes couldn't quite make out the face. He woke up the next morning with the dream still vivid in his mind.

11

SATURDAY MORNING AT the Blacklin County jail was pretty much the same as always. A good many drunks were in the cells, but they would all be gone by noon. No other crimes to speak of overnight, unless you counted the poisoned beer.

"Poisoned beer?" Rhodes asked Hack. "That's a new one on me."

"New one on all of us," Hack said. "Jack Turner, down on the Bellem Road, found a six pack of Miller on his front steps about three o'clock when he got in from clubbin'. He figured nobody'd leave a six pack on his porch 'less there was a good reason. He figured the best reason would be that it was poisoned."

"Considering how much he's probably had to drink by that time of the morning, I can see how he might come to that conclusion," Rhodes said.

"Yeah, I guess," Hack said. "But I don't take much to gettin' woke up at that time of mornin' to hear some drunk tellin' me about how somebody is tryin' to poison him with beer."

"So what came of it?" Rhodes asked.

"Not much. Turns out some fella down the road from Turner had borrowed a six pack off him a week or so back and just returned it. Since nobody was home, he just left it on the steps. Turner recalled that about the time he got home and called the guy."

"He come back?"

Hack laughed. "He surely did. He was so afraid we'd send

the stuff off to be analyzed that he came back to get it. I 'spect it's been drunk by now. Anyway, it'll never last till night."

Rhodes agreed. He checked a few reports and decided to take another trip to Thurston. He was just about to leave when Billy Don Painter walked in.

Billy Don Painter was the nearest thing to a hotshot lawyer in Blacklin County. He'd graduated from the law school at Austin and managed to pass the bar on his second try. A couple of times early in his career he'd gotten lucky with juries and managed to get a couple of men off when nearly everyone had thought he didn't have a prayer. Ever since, he'd had the reputation of the man to get if you were really in trouble or if you wanted to win a big suit.

Women seemed to find him attractive, or maybe it was his money they liked. At any rate, he'd been married three times to progressively younger brides. The current one was about twenty-three. Billy Don was close to fifty himself.

No one in Clearview had ever seen Billy Don Painter without a jacket and tie. He didn't buy the suits locally, either. They were expensive and conservative. His ties always matched. He was tall and trim and looked good in his clothes. He'd always reminded Rhodes of a tall James Mason, with a Texas drawl.

"Mornin', Sheriff," he said as he strolled into the jail. He always entered a room as if he owned it and anyone else there was merely visiting. "How you-all doin' this fine day?"

"I'm fine, Mr. Painter," Rhodes said. "What can we do for you?"

"Not me, Sheriff, not me. You can do nothin' for me. It's my client, Mr. Terry Wayne, for whom you can do something."

Rhodes had known it was coming as soon as Painter had stepped in the door. Painter hadn't had a hot case in nearly a year now, and a good police brutality contest would get him back in the public eye, where he loved to be.

"And what is it I can do for poor Mr. Wayne?" Rhodes asked.

"Why you can give him justice. Fire that brutal deputy of yours and see to it that the county recompenses Mr. Wayne for the terrible physical suffering that he has undergone."

"He looked pretty healthy to me the other night," Rhodes said.

"That was before I had him examined by a doctor," Painter said. "He has suffered serious internal injury to his vitals, and this county is responsible."

"Well, I guess that could be a matter of opinion," Rhodes said. "I guess the county could hire a doctor, too."

"You had better do so, then," Painter told him. "I am on my way at this moment to the office of the district attorney to file charges against you, your deputy, and the commissioners of this county. Unless we can come to some settlement, of course."

"Of course," Rhodes said. "Naturally you've consulted with the commissioners about this."

"Naturally," Painter said.

Fine, Rhodes thought. That's just fine. He wondered why the telephone wasn't ringing at that very moment. He didn't say anything, however.

Painter stood and looked at Rhodes for a second or two. Then he turned to go. "See you in court, Sheriff," he said.

Not if I see you first, Rhodes thought, then chided himself for acting like an adolescent. Still, he couldn't bring himself to respond.

After the lawyer had left, Hack broke the silence. "Never a dull moment," he said. "Hard to remember what I did for fun before I took up this here law enforcement career."

"I'm glad the county could help you out," Rhodes said.

It was funny how big things could drive little things out of your mind. Rhodes hadn't even thought about the robbery of

Hod Barrett's store until he drove up to the door. It would make a good excuse to begin his talk with Hod.

Barrett was inside, counting out change for a customer. ". . . And twenty-five makes a dollar," he said, putting a quarter into the hand of a woman in a cotton print dress. "You come again, now, Miz Barney."

"I will, Mr. Barrett," the woman responded, picking up the small brown sack that held her purchases. She stepped by Rhodes without noticing him.

It was quiet in the store, especially for a Saturday morning. There was no one on the loafer's bench, and no one else in the store. "Where is everybody?" Rhodes asked.

"That damn Safeway in Clearview is havin' a big sale," Barrett said. "Won't be anybody in here today unless they run out of bread or milk. I might just as well close up."

"Can't be that bad," Rhodes said.

"Bad enough," Barrett said. "At least I ain't been robbed in a day or two, though."

Given his opening, Rhodes asked, "Tell me a little bit more about that robbery, Hod. What with Jeanne getting killed and all, I really didn't get to ask you everything I needed to know."

"What else could I tell you?" Hod asked. "You saw the break-in. I told you what was taken."

"You didn't tell me exactly what was taken," Rhodes said. "You just said 'smokes and beers,' as I remember it."

Barrett came out from behind the counter and led Rhodes to the back of the store. In front of the stacks of Northern tissue was an opened case of Merit Menthol 100s. "Got about six cartons out of here," Barrett said. "They got a few six packs of Lone Star, too. As far as I can tell, that's all they got. Like I said, probably just some kids out to get somethin' for free."

"Probably," Rhodes said. "By the way, Hod, where were you yesterday morning? I came in here to use your telephone, and Larry Bell was minding the store."

"He does that for me every now and then," Hod said, "I had to go to the house for a minute, and I was deliverin' an order or two. I'm not like a Safeway. If my customers can't come to me, I'll go to them. Not that that keeps them from going to Clearview when they have the time."

It sounded likely, and it might even be true, Rhodes thought. "Have you talked to your wife about your going over to the Clintons' house?" he asked.

Hod brought up his hands, then jammed them in his pockets. "I don't want to talk to you about that no more, Sheriff. I said more than I ever wanted to say already. You got to believe that has nothing to do with me or my wife now. Jeanne's dead, and I'm sorry. Real sorry. But now I got to go on and maybe find somebody else to talk to. But that somebody won't be my wife."

"I may need to talk to her again," Rhodes said.

"You just go right ahead, Sheriff. I expect you've done all the damage you can do me in that way," Barrett told him.

"Before I do," Rhodes said, "there's one more thing I'd like to ask you. Think about it before you say anything, because it won't be obvious. If it was, you'd already have told me. But did you ever see anyone else at Jeanne's when you went there? Or maybe somebody just hanging around there at night?"

Barrett shook his head. "Never."

"Are you sure? There were others there from time to time, whether you knew it or not. Bill Tomkins certainly knew it."

Barrett jerked his hands from his pockets. "That damn silly Tomkins didn't have no more sense than a possum eatin' persimmons. He told all kinds of tales here in the store about one thing or another, but nobody ever paid him no mind."

"I believe he was telling the truth about this," Rhodes said. "One man he saw has already admitted it . . . besides you, I mean. He was telling the truth about you, too. Come to think of it, your wife may have heard about you from Tomkins."

"That's enough of that, Sheriff," Barrett said. "Plumb

enough. I got a store to run here, and you ain't helpin'. I never saw anybody around Jeanne's, and that's that. Bill Tomkins was a gossip and a fool, and anybody else in town would tell you the same." He stepped around Rhodes and went back to the front of the store.

Rhodes watched him go. The screen doors opened, and someone came in, handing Barrett an order list which he started to fill by going around to the shelves on the left wall. Rhodes went on out the back door.

The cooler was still on the ground where it had fallen. Hod probably hadn't had time to get his wife to build a new stand for it. Rhodes looked at the opening thoughtfully. Someone had nailed boards to the window facing from the inside. Maybe Barrett had done that himself.

Rhodes wondered about who had broken in. Kids, young kids, would have taken more candy than anything, and teen-agers would have taken a lot more beer. Hungry people would have taken food.

Rhodes began to feel that he was looking at a jigsaw puzzle, with the pieces scattered all over a table. If he could just push the pieces around until they began to look like something, he might be able to assemble them. In fact, his mind was pushing them around right now, and he wasn't too pleased with the picture that he thought might result when the assembly was done. He kicked at the wooden frame. It was time for him to go see James Allen.

James Allen lived on one of the county roads between Clearview and Thurston in a house like the one that Jack built. Allen had started out in a small five-room house when he'd first married, and then he and his wife had begun having children on a yearly basis. They'd stopped after seven, but Allen had kept adding rooms onto the sides and back of his house for years. Anyone familiar with the original dwelling could still discern part of the front of the house, but that was about all.

Allen had been a bulldozer operator who had gone into partnership with his brother and soon found himself making a lot of money in heavy equipment jobs. He needed the money to finance his housing additions, but within a few years he was making a comfortable living even beyond his basic needs. That was when he decided to run for county commissioner.

People in the country around Clearview knew him and liked him, and he won his precinct handily. He and Rhodes had gone to school together, played football together, and even dated some of the same girls. He was Rhodes's best friend among the commissioners.

He was mowing his front yard as Rhodes drove up.

"Can't you get one of the boys to do that?" Rhodes asked as he stepped out of his car.

Allen grinned and killed the mower. "I need the exercise," he said. "Besides, all those boys are too tired after being out half the night chasing girls. What can I do for you, Dan?"

"I guess you've heard about that Terry Wayne hiring Billy Don Painter," Rhodes said.

"Yep. Heard it from the man himself," Allen said. "Let's us go sit down."

They walked over to two aluminum lawn chairs webbed with colorful green and yellow plastic strips. The chairs were situated under a tall pecan tree, but the sun had shifted since they were placed there. Rhodes and Allen each took a chair and moved it back nearer the trunk of the tree, into the patchy shade of its branches. Rhodes sat and took a deep breath. He loved the smell of new-mown grass, especially if he hadn't had to mow it himself.

"What do you think will happen?" Rhodes said.

"The usual," Allen responded. "The judge will call a special meeting of the commissioners, and we'll all piss and moan about the situation, and then we'll support the sheriff's department one hundred percent just like we always do."

Rhodes laughed. "Yeah, I know how that support goes. It

sounds fine in the paper, but off the record I'm going to get my butt chewed."

"Off the record you probably will. There's two or three men who don't think too much of Johnny Sherman, and they weren't happy when he hired on with the department. They may use this little scrape as an excuse to get his job."

"There's never been any question about his work before," Rhodes said stiffly.

"I know that, and so does the rest of the court," Allen said, "but some of them remember when Johnny was a kid. He had a few problems back then. Little things, mostly, but there were one or two times when things got more serious."

"That must've been when I was out of the county, then," Rhodes said. "I never heard about them. Not even privately."

"They weren't the kind of things anybody'd want to bring up, exactly," Allen told him. "In fact, you could kind of say they were covered up, in a way."

"What kind of way?"

"The kind of way things always get covered up. Johnny was a good ball player, and the team was in the district race. So what if he got into a few fights? It's true that the other boys involved never wanted to press charges, and that they even refused to say that Johnny started the fights when it came right down to it, but one of them was beat up pretty bad. He was on the football team too, but he was only a second-stringer, so nobody worried too much about him except maybe his folks. He didn't play any more ball that year, that's for sure."

Rhodes tipped his chair back and thought about what Allen had said. "Why didn't anybody tell me this when Johnny came around about a job?"

"Letting bygones be bygones, I guess you could say. Giving Johnny a chance to show he'd changed."

"But now we've got some people who're thinking he hasn't changed, and they'll be saying that they knew all along he was no good. They'll be saying they tried all along to keep me from hiring him." Rhodes sighed. He'd been through things like this before, on a smaller scale. It was a part of his job that he didn't like, any more than he liked slapping backs and shaking hands, the kind of things that Ralph Claymore was so good at. Maybe Claymore would make a better sheriff than I do, at that, Rhodes thought.

"It won't be as bad as all that," Allen said. "At least I hope it won't. If we can just prove that Johnny didn't start that fight and that Terry Wayne and his buddy are just two drunks lookin' to take the county for some money in a false suit, everything will be all right."

"And if we can't prove that?" Rhodes asked.

"Don't even think like that, especially out loud," Allen said. "It's bad luck."

Rhodes got out of his chair. "You're right," he said. "I've got to have a positive attitude. Thanks for talking to me, James."

Allen stood and put out his hand, which Rhodes shook. "Don't worry about it," Allen said. "Everything will work out fine."

"I know," Rhodes said as he started for his car. "I won't worry about it."

But of course he did.

12

THE COUNTY COURTHOUSE had always looked to Rhodes like a smaller version of the Kremlin, but he'd never mentioned the resemblance to anyone. He wasn't sure there was anyone in Blacklin County who could appreciate the irony. He liked the old building himself, and he hated to think what might happen to it if some of the good citizens of the county started trying to give it a facelift to remove any suspected communist influence.

He walked up the broad walk under the shading pecan trees, up the wide front steps past the usual crowd of courthouse loafers, and through the pneumatic glass doors which were one of the only modern features of the building. They had been added a few years back when the building had been air-conditioned, and Rhodes still regretted both additions—the doors and the air-conditioning. With its thick stone walls and twelve-foot ceilings, the courthouse had always seemed to him cool and comfortable even in the summertime.

His shoe heels struck echoes from the marble floors as he walked down the hall to the stairs. He mounted the stairs, turned left into a corridor much narrower than the main halls, and came to his own private office. Like most sheriffs of Blacklin County, Rhodes spent most of his time either at the jail or on the road. No one ever called the courthouse office without calling the jail first, and no one ever came by the office looking for the sheriff because he was never there. Unless, of course, he wanted to be alone.

Rhodes wanted to be alone. The Terry Wayne business had him worried, and the two murders in Thurston had him even more worried. Allen hadn't mentioned the murders. After all, there was no real pressure from the murders yet. Jeanne Clinton and Bill Tomkins weren't from prominent families, so the county fathers weren't taking any particular interest in them. But Rhodes knew that the murders were being talked about, and they certainly bothered him. He didn't like for things to happen in his county unless he could take care of them.

He unlocked the door to his office. The top half was of pebbled glass, with the words "County Sheriff" somehow inlaid in gold letters. Rhodes's name was not on the door, which saved the county the expense of changing glass after elections. That reminded Rhodes of his own prospects in the upcoming election. Obviously two unsolved murders were not helping him, not to mention the Terry Wayne case. Besides, Ralph Claymore was an imposing opponent, and Rhodes felt honor bound not to mention Claymore's involvement with Jeanne Clinton unless it became apparent that the involvement was more than it seemed at present.

Rhodes walked over to a sagging leather office chair behind a completely bare oak desk. He sank into the chair, leaned back, and put his feet up on the desk top, which was inlaid with scratched and scarred black leather. Probably scarred by a lot of feet propped on it rather than a lot of hard work, Rhodes thought.

He wondered briefly how Ralph Claymore would be at investigating a crime like the murder of Jeanne Clinton. Whereas Rhodes had done most of the work himself, questioning everyone who looked as if he might be involved, Claymore would probably have laid all that kind of thing off on the deputies, preferring to talk to the judge and the commissioners, clapping them on the backs and assuring them that everything was being taken care of. Claymore could be very convincing, with his confident voice and manner. Even if he never caught the killer, he'd have the commissioners believing he had, and the whole thing would blow over in a week or two. By then, everyone would have forgotten all about it. It wasn't the first time Rhodes had wished he could have a little of Claymore in himself, but he didn't, and that was that.

Johnny Sherman was another problem. He'd offered to resign, of course, and of course Rhodes had turned him down. One of Rhodes's many faults was his loyalty to the men who worked for him. If he could take the heat instead of passing it along to them, he took the heat. If he could put himself in as a buffer between them and public opinion, he put himself in. He'd never been sorry in the past, but things were beginning to look different to him this time. There were a number of troubling signs, none of them big enough in themselves to call for Rhodes to change his mind about his policies, but taken together they were certainly beginning to look bothersome.

Rhodes got up from the desk and went back out into the hall. He took some change out of his pocket and headed for the Dr Pepper machine. It was the only machine in town, as far as Rhodes knew, that still held bottled drinks in returnable bottles. There was a rack beside it which held two wooden soft-drink cases partially filled with empties. He put in his change, pushed the button, and picked up his bottle. It was somehow much more satisfying to hold a cool, moisture-beaded bottle than an aluminum can. He opened the bottle and went back to his office.

It was very quiet in the old building, even for a Saturday. Rhodes thought that he might be the only person there. From his office he couldn't hear the old men loafing around the front door. He took a drink from his Dr Pepper and sat back down in his chair.

Rhodes sat for quite a while, drinking his drink and enjoying the silence. He hardly thought about the various problems that confronted him, at least he hardly thought about them consciously. He thought about his daughter, and he thought about Ivy Daniels, both of whom were much more pleasant to contemplate than murder and assault. Finally he called Hack.

There were no problems at the jail, nothing that required the immediate attention of the High Sheriff of Blacklin County.

Rhodes removed his feet from his desk and went home.

Clearview was one of the few towns of any size at all that still had no franchise hamburger stands. No MacDonald's. No Burger King. No Wendy's. This was just fine with Rhodes, who did not want something that you had to order by a number or by some funny name. When he went out for a hamburger, he wanted a hamburger—a bun, a meat patty, pickles, mustard, onions, and lettuce—and he wanted to order a hamburger. You could get a hamburger nearly anywhere in Clearview, but Rhodes took Ivy Daniels to the Bluebonnet Cafe because the owner was a friend of his.

"Cafe" was probably too fancy a name for the Bluebonnet, to tell the truth. It was nothing more than a ramshackle wooden building that contained one big room to eat in and a kitchen separated from the room by a high counter. There were no fancy plants, and probably none could have survived the atmosphere of the Bluebonnet, which had a high grease content. Rhodes didn't mind that, either. A real hamburger was, by definition, a little greasy. There were a lot of old wooden tables and benches—no chairs—scattered around the room. Several men in working clothes sat at the tables drinking beer from long-necked bottles. They hadn't bothered to remove their gimme caps.

Everyone looked up when Rhodes and Ivy Daniels entered. One man waved a hand idly, then went back to his beer. "It's not exactly Jeoff's, is it?" Rhodes said.

"Not exactly," Ivy said, but she clearly didn't care. She walked over to one of the benches. "Let's sit here. I'll have a hamburger all the way. Do you want to split an order of fries?"

"Sure," Rhodes said. He was feeling slightly giddy. He'd decided to bring Ivy to the Bluebonnet as a sort of a test. He didn't know exactly what he'd been trying to prove, but whatever it was, Ivy had passed without question. She hadn't even asked him to get salad dressing on her hamburger. She hadn't even asked him to cut the onions. She was almost too good to be true.

Rhodes walked over to the high counter, which came almost up to his shoulders. "Hey, Sheriff, how you doin'?" the cafe's owner asked. Lonnie Eslick was a short man with a crew cut. If there hadn't been a raised platform behind the counter, only his crew cut would have been visible.

"Fine, Lonnie, just fine. Give me two hamburgers all the way and an order of fries."

"Comin' right up, Sheriff. I'll call you," Eslick said. He disappeared from view as he stepped down off the platform and went back into the kitchen.

Rhodes walked back to the table and sat on the bench across from Ivy Daniels. She grinned at him. "Come here often, Sheriff?" she asked.

He smiled back. "Often enough to know this is the place with the best burgers in Clearview. You said the other night that a hamburger would be fine, so here we are. I hope you weren't kidding."

"I wasn't kidding," she assured him. "I like a good hamburger as well as anyone. To tell the truth, I'd just as soon have a good burger as that tenderloin."

Rhodes found himself not knowing what to say next. It struck him suddenly that he was too old to be out on a date, and he felt awkward.

If Ivy sensed his feeling, it didn't show. The brief silence didn't seem to bother her at all. She let it lengthen for a minute, then spoke again. "How is your investigation going?" she asked. "Have you cracked the case yet?" She laughed. "Or do real lawmen really say things like 'crack the case'?"

Rhodes laughed too. "I don't know about 'real lawmen,' " he said. "I do know that nobody around the sheriff's department is likely to say anything like that. That could all change, though, if Ralph Claymore is elected. I expect he'll require everybody to talk like they talk on television."

The conversation went smoothly after that, with Rhodes telling Ivy about what he'd been doing and about the lack of progress. "Of course, the second killing hasn't made it any easier," he added.

"I'll just bet," Ivy said. "Nothing is ever as easy or as simple as it should be." She then launched into some funny stories about the hazards of running for justice of the peace. There had even been a letter about her in the Clearview *Herald,* which Rhodes hadn't read.

"Well, you should have read it," Ivy told him. "It was a classic. Really, it's hard to believe that people could believe such things, especially in 1986."

The letter had been from a woman who objected to Ivy's campaign. The woman felt that it was a fine thing to live in a free country, where women had the right to do as they pleased; but she thought that it was a shame that some women were pleased to run for public office. She knew that she, as a mere woman, would hate to be put in a position where she might have to make a decision that reflected unfavorably on a man, one of those creatures that God had clearly intended as her superiors. For her part, she was quite content to cook and clean for her husband, as every woman should do in the natural order of things.

"Honestly, I almost felt guilty after I read it," Ivy said, laughing. "I wondered if I were doing the wrong thing. Thank goodness I came to my senses before I resigned my job and gave up my campaign."

Rhodes laughed with her, then got up and walked over to the counter in response to Eslick's call. "Burgers up, Sheriff!"

The hamburgers were warm in their grease-spotted paper wrappers, and the wedge-shaped home fries almost burned Rhodes's fingers through the thin cardboard of their box. He hustled them back to the table, almost overwhelmed by the smell. He hoped that his mouth wasn't watering.

Ivy again impressed him. She made no small talk but went right about unwrapping her burger and taking a healthy bite, and he followed suit. Plenty of mustard, just the right amount of sweet white onion, and a generous portion of fried meat. It was probably terrible for your heart, but it did the soul good. Rhodes took a paper napkin from the holder on the table, wiped his mouth, and continued eating.

Only then did he remember that he'd forgotten to order drinks. He was saved embarrassment by Eslick, who came to the table carrying two large paper cups.

"Dr Pepper, right?" Eslick asked.

"Thanks, Lonnie," Rhodes said. "I guess I was in a hurry to eat."

The short counterman grinned. "That's fine with me. I always take it as a compliment when someone wants to eat my cookin'."

"These really are delicious hamburgers," Ivy said.

Eslick didn't quite blush. "Thank you, ma'am," he said, then scurried back behind his counter.

After they had eaten, Rhodes and Ivy drove around Clearview. Ivy brought up the killings once more. "What about Ralph Claymore?" she asked, referring to the information she had given Rhodes earlier. "Don't tell me if you think I shouldn't know," she added hurriedly. "I don't want you to gossip about your job. It's just that I'm curious about what I'd heard."

"There's no confidential information involved," Rhodes said. "I don't think Claymore had anything to do with Jeanne's death, but you were right. He *had* been seeing her." He went on to tell her about Hod Barrett, Barrett's wife, and Elmer Clinton's grief.

"I'll bet Hod Barrett did it," Ivy said. "The way you describe him, I can almost see it. Why, I think he could even have staged the robbery of his store to put you off, to make you think of something else instead of him."

"That's possible, I guess," Rhodes said. "I've thought about it. And of course Mrs. Barrett's an unusual woman." He had mentioned only Mrs. Barrett's cleaning habits, not her views of sex.

"She surely is," Ivy agreed. "Anyone who is that clean must be putting a lot of energy into house and yard work to avoid putting it somewhere else. If she directed it toward Jeanne Clinton, who knows what might have happened? She sounds a lot like the woman who wrote that letter I mentioned."

Rhodes figured that he knew exactly what energy Mrs. Barrett was putting into her physical labor, but he didn't say anything. He wasn't quite ready to talk with Ivy about intimate things like that. He changed the subject. "How did you ever get a name like Ivy?" he asked.

She looked at him. "What?"

"How did you get a name like Ivy? I mean, I like it. It's a nice, old-fashioned name. These days I find myself having to deal with grown women named 'Fawn' or 'Sharamee.' Not long ago I had to deal with one named 'Rainbeau.' " He spelled it. "I'm not making this up," he added.

Ivy laughed. "I believe you," she said. "Remember, I work in an insurance office. I've probably heard a few that you haven't heard."

"For example?"

"How about 'Winsey'?"

" 'Winsey'?"

"Her father's name is 'Winston,' " Ivy said.

"OK, but I still think 'Rainbeau' wins the prize," Rhodes said. He noticed that somehow Ivy had gotten closer to him. In fact, she was very close. Feeling almost like a teenager, Rhodes put his arm around her, and his heart chugged as she settled against him.

* * *

118

Rhodes woke up the next morning thinking that it was a good thing he was no longer a teenager, even if he had briefly felt like one. As he remembered his teenage years, the hormones, or whatever they were, had been coursing through his veins at such a rate that Ivy Daniels would not have been safe within half a mile of him. As it was, he didn't know exactly what he might be getting himself into. He knew that he had strong feelings for Ivy, but he didn't know just what she felt about him. Oh, she liked him. That much was pretty clear. But whether she was beginning to think of him as something more than just a friend was a question that Rhodes couldn't answer.

Still, he could hardly keep a sort of half-grin off his face as Kathy scrambled eggs for their breakfast. It was to her credit, he reflected, that she said nothing at all about it.

After breakfast, he called the jail to check in and found that nothing out of the ordinary had happened overnight; everything was under control, and there was no need for him to go in. He could relax, read his Sunday paper, and think about the bad part of the afternoon ahead. Hack had told him that the autopsy on Jeanne had been completed—she had died of a broken neck and had not been raped. Her funeral would be that afternoon at two o'clock.

Even the thought of the funeral didn't bother Rhodes. For some reason, he had the confident feeling that things were going to start going his way and that the case would take a turn for the better soon.

He was wrong, however. That afternoon at the funeral, all hell broke loose.

13

THINGS STARTED OUT as well as anyone could expect. The church service, held at the Thurston Baptist Church, was quietly dignified. Only one hymn was sung, "A Mighty Fortress Is Our God," which surprised Rhodes. He hadn't thought anyone in Thurston, particularly Elmer Clinton, had the good taste to choose something other than a traditional weeper like "The Old Rugged Cross." The minister painted Jeanne as a fine young woman, who if not a pillar of the church had at least "reformed" since her marriage to Elmer and had no longer sought the "bright lights and glamour" of the "world of the flesh," a reference which Rhodes took to mean that she'd given up participating in wet T-shirt contests at the Paragon.

The mourners, of which there were a goodly number for Thurston (about fifty in Rhodes's estimation), were silent and respectful. In the pews near the back were Hod Barrett and his wife. Rhodes recognized Larry Bell and a few others as well. Elmer sobbed quietly and alone in the front pew.

It was at the graveside that things got bad. The rain had made digging easy, and Rhodes could see the backhoe machine parked at a discreet distance behind some trees at the edge of the Thurston cemetery. The mound of muddy earth scooped from the grave was covered with something resembling Astroturf. The mourners were seated under an open-sided tent in wooden folding chairs. Almost everyone from the church had come to the cemetery.

Elmer's sobbing was louder in the tent, and the vague outdoor sounds of the wind in the trees and the insects in the grass did nothing to drown him out. The minister seemed to have decided to make up for the lack of sentimentality in the previous service by making his opening remarks about "a beautiful young woman, struck down in the prime of her life," at which a number of women began digging in their purses for tissues and handkerchiefs. One of the women so engaged was Mrs. Barrett.

Then the minister made a few remarks related to the scriptures, about returning to dust and the sun also rising and the sun going down. Several of the women, and Elmer, were weeping openly.

Rhodes looked at the casket sitting over the open grave on the belts that would be used to lower it. Elmer was walking toward it, and it was only then that Rhodes realized that this was going to be one of those funerals in which the casket was lowered in full view of the mourners and in which the deceased's husband was going to throw on the first clods of earth. Rhodes understood the theory—it would be a definite parting, shocking the husband into the realization that life must go on and his dead wife could no longer be a part of it. He understood the theory, all right, but he didn't necessarily approve of it.

The coffin was lowered slowly and expertly into the ground by two men from the funeral home who had been standing quietly by in their black suits, looking for all the world like any other mourners there.

Elmer worked a clump of the damp black earth in his hands as the tears streamed down his face. "I love you, Jeanne," he said in a choked voice, so quietly that Rhodes could hardly hear. "I'll never forget you." He crumbled the dirt in his hands and tossed it into the grave, then stood silently looking down.

It was a dramatic moment, and Mrs. Barrett couldn't have chosen it better if she had been Cecil B. DeMille. She leaped out of her chair, slamming it into a stout woman in black who sat behind her. The stout woman may have cried out, but if she did Rhodes didn't hear her. All he could hear was Mrs. Barrett, yelling at the top of her lungs. "The Whore of Babylon!" she shrieked. "The Scarlet Whore of Babylon!" Apparently she hadn't bought the minister's picture of a reformed Jeanne Clinton after all. She'd been crying about something else.

After her first outburst, Mrs. Barrett ran amok. Rhodes was pretty sure that he'd never seen anyone run amok before, but that was about the only way to describe Mrs. Barrett. She ran crashing through the mourners, knocking chairs right and left, and knocking a few of the less agile mourners right and left as well. Once she leaped into the air. Had she flapped her arms, she might have taken flight.

The minister was paralyzed. Like Rhodes, he'd never seen anything to resemble what was going on. Mrs. Barrett didn't stop for him. She bowled him over and kept on going. She came to an abrupt stop at the edge of the open grave, yelling down at the coffin.

"You lured the men with your skimpy clothes and your painted face," she yelled. "But you never gave them what you promised. A teaser, that's what you were, and now you're dead! Killed by Hod Barrett, that you lured from his proper bed, and serves you right!"

She worked her throat, and Rhodes was horrified that she was about to spit into the grave. He finally managed to get himself into action, at just about the same time as Hod Barrett. Elmer Clinton had started for her first, a strangled cry ripping from his throat, but when she had named Hod as the killer, Clinton had changed course and made for Hod.

Rhodes didn't know which way to go. Clinton had collided with Barrett and had his hands wrapped around his throat. Barrett had Clinton in a bear hug and was squeezing for all he was worth. At the edge of the grave Mrs. Barrett was hopping around. Her shoe heel caught in the soft earth and her right leg gave way beneath her. She started to fall into the grave.

Out of the corner of his eye, Rhodes saw Larry Bell start

for Mrs. Barrett, so he went for Clinton and Barrett. The two men had also lost their footing and were rolling around in the chairs already knocked over by Barrett's wife. Women were screaming and trying to get out of the way. Men were yelling and cursing; a couple of them tried to reach into the whirling mass that Barrett and Clinton had become. One of them got a huge fist in his eye and fell aside. The other backed off and stepped aside for Rhodes.

The two men rolled forward. The minister sat up and watched them dazedly. Rhodes tried to grab Clinton's jacket, but his hand slipped. The men rolled up against the pile of dirt from the grave and somehow struggled to their feet. Clinton slammed Barrett into the Astroturf.

Barrett fell against the carpet. Struggling to stand again, he pulled a section of it off the dirt it covered. When Clinton plowed into him, both men smacked into the wet earth. They pummeled each other, the dirt, and the air.

Rhodes knew of only one thing to do, so he did it. He was wearing his .38 in a discreet holster at the back of his belt where it was covered by the coat to his suit. He pulled it out and fired it three times. It put an end to the fight, and it shocked everyone into a complete and utter silence. No one there had ever heard a pistol fired at a funeral before. Most of them would talk about this occasion for the rest of their lives.

Rhodes looked at Barrett and Clinton. They were covered with mud and grass stains, red-faced and sweaty. He looked over at Mrs. Barrett. Larry Bell was holding her hand as she sat at the edge of the grave, one leg dangling over, her carefully pinned hair all disarranged around her face. The minister was up and going over to her.

Rhodes considered Barrett carefully, arranging the puzzle pieces in his mind, trying to make them fit. "I guess you're under arrest, Hod," he said.

Barrett was panting and breathing through his mouth. "You'd take the word of a crazy woman?" he asked. "You know she's not right in the head. You can't arrest me!"

"I guess I have to, Hod. Everyone here heard her accuse you. It wouldn't look right if I just let you go. We can just say I'm taking you in for questioning. Then we can talk to your wife after she's calmed down some. If she wants to change her story, that's fine. We'll see what evidence she's got against you."

"You'd damned sure better take him in, Sheriff," Elmer Clinton said. "You don't, and he's a dead man." Clinton was as winded as Barrett, but he sounded convincing. His eyes were narrowed and his voice was shaky with anger as well as fatigue.

"The Whore of Babylon!" Mrs. Barrett shouted. Elmer Clinton's shoulders tightened, and his hands formed claws. "Take that bitch, too," he said.

"Watch your language, Elmer," Rhodes told him. "Have a little dignity at your wife's funeral." He turned toward Mrs. Barrett. "Come on, Hod," he said.

Larry Bell was patting Mrs. Barrett on the shoulder as Rhodes walked up. "Now, now, Mrs. Barrett," he was saying. "Jeanne wasn't no whore. I went to high school with that girl, known her ever since. She might of been wild at one time, but not no more."

The puzzle pieces shuffled themselves in Rhodes's mind once more. He didn't like the new arrangement any more than he'd liked the old one. "Can you get her home, Larry?" he asked.

Bell helped her to her feet, his hand under her elbow. "Sure," he said. "Be glad to."

"Thanks," Rhodes said. He led Barrett over to the county car and opened the back door. Barrett sighed and got in. Rhodes got in the front, started the car, and drove away. He looked in the rearview mirror. The mourners were beginning to head for their cars, the ones that weren't still waving their hands and talking. The minister was making no effort to call them back. For all practical purposes, the funeral of Jeanne Clinton was over.

Barrett had little to say on the way back to Clearview. It was only when they arrived at the jail that he began to talk. "You really going to arrest me?" he asked.

"Sure enough," Rhodes said. "But not for murder. Right now the charge will be more like 'disturbing the peace.' You were guilty of that, don't you think."

"Me and a few others," Barrett said.

Rhodes pulled up in front of the jail, got out of the car, and let Barrett out. "If you're innocent, you won't be in but overnight," Rhodes said. "In fact, if you call a lawyer you can get out sooner. Be damned hard to find a lawyer in Clearview on Sunday afternoon, though."

"I won't be needing a lawyer. And it won't hurt me to spend the night here," Barrett said. "The way Elmer's feeling, I might be better off here than at home."

"Now you're showing some sense," Rhodes said. They went inside.

After the formalities were taken care of, Lawton led Hod Barrett up to his cell.

"Think him and Billy Joe'll get along up there?" Hack asked.

"I expect so," Rhodes said. "Seen Johnny today?"

"This is his day off," Hack said. "He comes in sometimes, but not today. He hasn't had much to say lately, to tell the truth. Why?"

"Nothing much," Rhodes said. "A few things have been bothering me, that's all. I think I need to have a long talk with Mr. Sherman."

"If I see him, I'll tell him you're looking for him," Hack said.

"You do that," Rhodes said. "Meantime, I think I'll go look for him myself."

Johnny Sherman wasn't at home, however, and Rhodes went to his own house on the off chance that Kathy and Johnny had patched things up. Kathy was there, alone.

"How was the funeral?" she asked when Rhodes entered. She was eating popcorn—the real thing, made at home, not some flavored stuff like the kind Rhodes had gotten in a big can at Christmas from one of his cousins.

Rhodes took off his suit coat and hung it on a chair back. Then he scooped up a handful of the popcorn. "You wouldn't believe it if I told you," he said.

"Try me," she said severely. "Or no more popcorn."

Rhodes grabbed another handful and proceeded to give a slightly exaggerated but generally accurate account of the events at Jeanne Clinton's funeral.

"I know I shouldn't laugh," Kathy said, laughing. "I know it's not really funny. And that poor Mrs. Barrett. Do you suppose that she has any real idea about her husband and whether he's guilty?"

Rhodes scraped the bottom of the popcorn bowl, getting a few of the unpopped kernels along with the good ones. "I thought she might, at first," he said. "Then I got another idea that I want to check out. I'll talk to her again tomorrow and see if she's just batty or if she has some information that I can really use."

"Not to change the subject," Kathy said, "but I've put out some steaks to thaw for supper, and there's plenty for three. You could cook them on the grill, and we could ask Ivy Daniels to join us. I'll bet she'd like to hear that story about the funeral."

Rhodes was hesitant. "I don't know about that," he said. "She's too much of a lady to laugh about a funeral."

"I laughed," Kathy pointed out.

"I didn't mean it that way," Rhodes said. "I just meant that, well, maybe we ought not to rush things with Ivy. I don't want to seem too pushy, and . . . uh . . .." He couldn't think of how to end his sentence.

"You *do* like her, don't you?" his daughter asked.

"Well, of course, but . . . I'm not really sure how she feels about me. After all, we've only seen each other a couple of times."

"I'll tell you what," Kathy said. "You get out of that monkey suit and find that apron you wear when you cook outside. I'll do the calling. I won't make her feel obligated. I can be very tactful when I try. If she turns me down, I can always call Mrs. Wilkie. I'll bet she could get herself over here in a New York minute."

"You wouldn't dare," Rhodes said.

"Don't be too sure. Anyway, I'll bet Ivy will not only come over, she'll also laugh at the story about the funeral."

"If she doesn't laugh, will you do the dishes?"

"I *always* do the dishes."

"And a good thing, too," Rhodes said.

He was right. It was a good thing, because Ivy not only came, she laughed. But that was all right with Rhodes. He liked a woman with a sense of humor.

14

RHODES DIDN'T EVEN go by the jail the next morning. Sunday night was the quietest night of the week. It was almost impossible to get liquor or beer on a Sunday, so there were very few accidents or fights. Even the few burglars in the area seemed willing to take the day off. Too, he wanted to talk with Mrs. Barrett before questioning her husband. He doubted that a night in jail would do anything to soften Hod up, and if there was a chance that Mrs. Barrett could provide him with any solid information he wanted to get it.

As he pulled into the Barrett drive, he once more marveled at the way things were kept. Such neatness, while undoubtedly commendable from most standpoints, was foreign to him. He got out of the car and knocked at the door.

There was no answer. Rhodes waited about thirty seconds and knocked again. Still no answer. It was possible that Mrs. Barrett had taken some sort of medication after arriving at home. She had certainly been in a state that would seem to have called for something like that.

Rhodes knocked for a third time, much more loudly than before, at the same time calling Mrs. Barrett's name. When he still received no response, he opened the screen and tried the door knob. It didn't move. The door was locked.

Rhodes thought he might as well try the back door before disturbing the neighbors. He walked around the side of the house on the neatly trimmed lawn, hoping that he wasn't displacing any of the carefully manicured blades of grass beneath his feet.

The backyard was as meticulously cared for as the front.

Rhodes walked to a small screened-in porch and opened the door. Then he stepped inside. There was a wooden door leading from the porch to the kitchen. The top half of the door had a window in it, but Rhodes didn't try to peek past its curtains. He knocked loudly and called.

No one answered, and Rhodes tried the knob. Locked. He peeked in the crack between the curtains. He could see very little, but what he could see was more than enough. He stepped back, took off his left shoe, and smashed out the window, after which he reached in and unlocked the door.

Mrs. Barrett lay in the middle of her kitchen. There was a .30-.30 rifle on the floor beside her. Most of her head was gone. There was blood and other material on the ceiling, and on the walls. Even a little on the stove, and of course on the floor.

Rhodes looked around. No note was evident. He stepped carefully around the body and looked quickly through the house. There was nothing out of the ordinary that he could spot.

There was a wall phone in the bedroom. Rhodes picked it up and began making his calls.

Once again it was afternoon when Rhodes got back to the jail. He felt that it was his job to tell Hod Barrett about his wife. In a way it was Rhodes's fault that she was dead.

Rhodes spoke briefly to Hack, filling him in. Then he went up to Barrett's cell. Billy Joe was nearby, making not a sound. Barrett was making enough noise for both of them.

"Goddammit, Sheriff," he said. "How long you think you can keep me locked up like this? I may be just a dumb country storekeeper, but I know that I got as many rights as the next fella. I guess it's time I called me a lawyer and saw about suing the whole lot of you!"

Rhodes didn't answer. He opened Barrett's cell, not locking the door behind him, and went to sit on the bunk.

"You tellin' me I can go, leavin' the door open like that?" Barrett wasn't quite sure what was happening.

"You can go, Hod," Rhodes said, "but first you got to listen to what I have to say. You aren't going to like it, any more than I'm going to like saying it. Your wife's dead."

"Dead? What you mean, 'dead'? She was fine yesterday."

"She was in her kitchen, shot dead with a .30-.30. The rifle was right there on the floor by her. You have a rifle like that, Hod?" Rhodes asked.

Barrett couldn't quite take it in. He sat beside Rhodes on the bunk. "Yeah, yeah, I got a gun like that. Winchester. Haven't fired it in years. Keep it behind the bedroom door. In case of break-ins at the house. A man's got a right to protect his house."

"Of course he does," Rhodes said. "I'd be willing to bet money that rifle's the same one used on Bill Tomkins, though. It won't take too long to find out."

Barrett's mind wasn't working in sequence. "Dead? My wife is dead? Shot in our own house?"

"That's right, Hod. I know how you must be feeling, and I know what you must think of me and my department. She's dead."

Barrett shook his head. "I don't believe it," he said. "This is some kind of cheap trick to get me to say something. Well, it won't work, because I got nothin' to say. I sure didn't kill Bill Tomkins, but even you can't be dumb enough to think I could kill my wife while I was locked up in your jail."

Rhodes shook his head. "No tricks," he said. "I wish it was a trick. She's really dead, Hod."

Barrett wrapped his huge hands around the edge of the mattress of the bunk and squeezed. "If she's dead, who killed her? Answer me that one."

"I think it was meant to look like she killed herself, Hod."

"With my gun? She didn't have no more idea how to use that gun than a chicken. She couldn't even have got the safety off," Barrett said with disgust.

"I said it was meant to look like she did it, not that I thought she did. Anybody who'd think Mrs. Barrett would mess up her kitchen just to kill herself didn't know your wife very well," Rhodes said. "I only met her at home the two times, but I knew her well enough to know that much."

"We had our troubles," Barrett said, his voice cracking slightly, "but I never thought about her bein' dead. Good lord, Sheriff, how many more folks are goin' to get killed around here before you put a stop to it?"

"No more, if I can help it," Rhodes told him. "Could you identify that rifle of yours, Hod?"

Barrett gathered himself, pulling himself erect on the cot. "How do you mean? You mean officially? No way. I bought it off a fella at a flea market five or six years ago, the way I bet half the guns in this county get bought. There wasn't any recordin' of serial numbers that I can recall. There's probably guns like it all over Thurston."

"That's what I thought, and that's probably what the killer thought, too, if he switched his gun for yours like I think he might have done. But I meant unofficially. I expect you marked your gun some way. Most folks do that."

"Yeah, I did that," Hod said. "It's got a butt plate on it, and my initials are carved under the butt plate. Just take out the screws and check it. Ought to be an 'H. B.' under there if it's mine."

"I'll check it," Rhodes said.

"Who did it, Sheriff? You know who did it?"

"I thought I had a pretty good idea yesterday," Rhodes said. "At first I thought your wife might know something she hadn't told, but then I had another thought. Your wife doesn't fit into the pattern too well, but I guess she could be made to fit."

"Why are you sittin' here talkin' to me then?" Barrett asked. "Why ain't you out arrestin' the sonuvabitch that did it?"

"There's a big problem there," Rhodes said. "I can make

all the facts fit, but there's one thing I don't have. The important thing. I don't have one bit of *evidence*." He smacked his fist down on the thin mattress of the bunk. A faint cloud of dust motes rose in the air.

Barrett stood up to his full height, balled his fists, and worked his arms in the air. "Evidence my ass. You get me the man who did it and then we'll worry about evidence."

"That door's open right now, Hod," Rhodes said quietly, "but if you keep talking like that, I'll close it mighty damn quick. You know better than to say things like that."

"It's my wife that's been killed, Sheriff," Barrett said.

"It's too late to cry about that," Rhodes said. "You should have worried more about her when she was alive. Maybe none of this would have happened if you had."

Barrett looked at him. "What do you mean by that?"

"I don't know," Rhodes said. "Forget it. It's hard to say anybody is really at fault in something like this. It's my fault as much as yours, or as much as anyone's, I guess. I'd just like for you to calm down and stop thinking about going out there and righting wrongs. That's my job, and I'm the one to do it."

Barrett stepped back to the bunk and sat again. "Can I see her?" he asked.

"You can see her if you want to, but I think you'd be better off not doing it," Rhodes said. "I don't think it would be a good idea. I think maybe you ought to go on home. Hack can drive you back."

Barrett continued to sit on the bunk, staring at the floor. Rhodes got up and went out the cell door. "I'm leaving the door open, Hod," he said. "You can leave when you get ready to." He walked out and down the corridor, taking a last look back over his shoulder. Hod Barrett still sat, his shoulders moving slightly as if he were crying. In the next cell, Billy Joe Byron sat watching him, his eyes round.

Rhodes paused and looked at Billy Joe. If Billy Joe could get over his fear and start talking, things would probably work out, but that seemed unlikely. Rhodes was going to have to go with what he had, which was suspicion, hunch, and guesswork. Everything fit, but there wasn't enough to make a case with. He'd just have to see how far he could get by just talking, and maybe with lying a little.

He went on down the stairs. He hoped he was wrong, but he didn't see how he could be. There was no other answer that fit with the facts. Maybe some scientific crimefighter somewhere could have done better, could have come up with the answer quicker, but Rhodes didn't see how. The autopsy of Jeanne Clinton had told them nothing except how she'd been killed, which they'd known already. He had to find a rifle that fired the bullets that killed Bill Tomkins before he could pin that one on anybody, and now that he'd found it someone else was dead.

He reached the bottom of the stairs. "Hack, if Hod comes down and needs a ride home, you give him one. I'll be out for a while. But before I go, call the DPS lab and ask them to check under the butt plate on that rifle from Hod's house. See if there's any initials carved on the stock."

"Sure thing," Hack said. "I guess Lawton could handle the dispatchin' work while I'm gone." He turned to the phone.

There were no initials on the rifle stock. Rhodes hadn't expected that there would be.

"Where you headed, Sheriff?" Hack asked.

"I'm going to have a little talk with Johnny Sherman," Rhodes said, starting out the door.

15

JOHNNY SHERMAN LIVED only a few blocks away from Rhodes, in a smaller and older frame house. His car was parked in his drive, and Rhodes went to the door.

Johnny came and let him in. "Hey, Sheriff," he said. "I was just getting up and stirring around a little. Thought I might have a bite to eat and watch some TV before going on shift. Come on in."

Rhodes stepped into a small living room dominated by a twenty-five-inch RCA Colortrak set. There was a La-Z Boy recliner strategically placed so that its occupant could see the television set while leaning back in comfort. The only other furniture in the room consisted of an early American rocker of the kind that can often be bought on sale at major drugstore chain outlets, along with a small end table beside the recliner. The floor was covered with a cheap green linoleum that looked as if it might have been installed by an amateur. But the room was neat and clean, with no sign of sloppy bachelor-hood in evidence.

There was a small window-unit air conditioner in the room's only window, and it labored noisily. The room was dim and cool.

"Have a seat, Sheriff," Johnny said. "Let me get you something to drink. I think I've got a Dr Pepper."

Rhodes went over to the rocker and sat in it. He didn't rock. "We need to have a little talk, Johnny," he said.

"Sure thing, Sheriff." Johnny smiled apologetically. "Just let me go change into something presentable." He was dressed in a white V-neck T-shirt and faded blue jeans. He was barefoot. "It won't take me but a minute."

Rhodes started to protest, but before he could say anything Johnny had stepped through the doorway into the bedroom and out of Rhodes's sight.

"Go ahead and talk if you want to," Johnny called. "I can hear you all right."

"I'll wait," Rhodes said, leaning back in the rocker, trying to relax and organize his thoughts.

In about ten minutes, Johnny was back. He had put on his uniform pants and his black shoes, and combed his hair. He had his uniform shirt in his right hand. "Still kind of warm to me," he said. "I just had a bath before you drove up, and it got me pretty steamy. I'll put on the shirt in a minute if you don't mind."

"That's OK," Rhodes said, leaning forward in the rocker.

Johnny sat in the recliner, but he didn't put up the footrest. "So what did you want to tell me?"

"It's about Jeanne Clinton . . ." Rhodes began.

"I've been keeping my eyes open," Johnny said. He looked earnest and solemn. He leaned forward, resting his elbows on his knees and clasping his hands. The shirt lay in his lap. "I haven't noticed a thing. Tell you what I think, though, is that those break-ins at Hod Barrett's store are tied in to the murder." He waited expectantly for Rhodes to speak.

"How's that?" Rhodes asked. "How can you connect them?"

"Well, not with evidence or anything," Johnny said. "But I think it's transients. That big new power plant they're building down near Simmonsville? Uses that lignite coal to generate electricity? No telling how many folks that's brought into the area, and not all of them are the kind of folks we need around here, let me tell you. You ought to see how they live— little cracker-box trailers that you wouldn't think could hold two people, and they've got eight or ten in there."

Rhodes knew all about the power plant, which was in a

neighboring county. "I don't think somebody would drive all that way for a few cigarettes and beers," he said.

"They might to see Jeanne Clinton, though," Johnny said. "She was really something."

"I'd been wanting to ask you about that," Rhodes said. "Didn't you say you went to high school with her?"

"Yeah, I might have said that. We weren't good friends or anything like that, but we were in the same class."

Rhodes stood up. The rocker was not very comfortable to him. "It seems natural that a man might want to drive by some night to see how his old friend was doing," he said.

"Now wait a minute, Sheriff," Johnny said.

"No, Johnny, I've already waited too long," Rhodes said. "Let me say what I have to say, and then we'll see what you think about it."

"OK," Johnny said, leaning back in the recliner. "I'll listen."

"Good. Let's say you might have driven by to see Jeanne. You might not have even wanted to stop, but it would be easy to see that Elmer wasn't there. In fact, taking into account all the visitors that she had, I'd be surprised if you didn't see one or two of them at her house some night or the other."

"Not saying I did, Sheriff, but so what? If she had all those visitors like you say, why should I mention it?"

"Early on, it might not have made any difference," Rhodes said. "Later it did. When Jeanne was killed you surely should have mentioned it to me, especially if you knew any of them. It might have been important to me. But you didn't mention it."

"Next I guess you're going to tell me I robbed Hod Barrett's grocery store," Johnny said with a good-natured grin. "You know better than that, Sheriff. I can afford to buy beer."

"I'm sure you can," Rhodes said. "I don't think you robbed anybody. I think Billy Joe Byron robbed that store. When I picked him up, he smelled like a brewery, and he had enough Merit cigarettes stashed in his clothes to last him quite a while. I guess I know where he got 'em. You can rest easy on the robbery business."

"Meaning I can't rest easy on something else?" There was a hard edge in Johnny's voice, and he wasn't grinning anymore.

Rhodes sighed. "I should have figured it out sooner, but I trusted you. You were one of my men. You were dating my daughter. That's my only excuse. It was right there all the time."

"I don't follow you. What was right there?"

"That fight with Terry Wayne and his pal. They weren't lying. They were telling the truth. You were coming back in, and you needed some way to explain the scratches and the blood, even if there wasn't much. So you spotted those guys in the Paragon lot, stopped, and started a fight with them. You knew we'd all believe your side of it."

"I guess that makes me a pretty clever guy," Johnny said, a trace of a smile back on his face. "Even if it were true, which it isn't, it's still my word against theirs."

Rhodes walked behind the rocker and put his hands on the chair back. "Yeah, but they've got Billy Don Painter on their side, and I'm afraid that they've even got me on their side. Anyway, I don't know how many times you've washed the shirt you wore that night, but blood's mighty hard to get out. There might be enough left for the lab boys to type."

"That's pretty slim pickings to go to trial on."

"I'd have to agree with that. But of course that's not all. You and I both know there was a witness to whatever happened in Jeanne Clinton's house that night. I'm beginning to wonder just how many witnesses there were. They must have been lined up three deep."

For the first time Johnny Sherman betrayed surprise. "You're really getting over my head now, Sheriff. Three deep? Why haven't all these witnesses come forward?"

Rhodes shoved down on the rocker, causing it to slide a bit on the linoleum floor. "Because two of them are dead. You missed the third one, though."

"You're crazy," Johnny said, and Rhodes was taken slightly aback. He'd been sure of his man, as sure as he could be without hard evidence, but Johnny sounded convincing. He really didn't seem to know what Rhodes meant.

Rhodes thought for a minute. "Let's start with Billy Joe," he said. "Lawton didn't leave that cell door open. You opened it. I'd bet you even led Billy Joe right down to the door to the office. Then you got out that magazine with the spicy pictures in it and showed it to Hack and Lawton. A little loud talking and laughing, and Billy Joe could be out the front door and on his way home, which was the only place he knew to go."

"Billy Joe saw me at Jeanne's, right? So I let him out of jail? You'll have to do better than that, Sheriff. It just doesn't make sense."

"It makes sense all right. Billy Joe's never been scared of me in his life, but he ran from me that morning I picked him up. It wasn't me he was running from. It was the uniform and the car. He thought I was you. We'd picked him up for window peeping a few years back. I guess he was doing it again. But this time he saw something he didn't bargain for. He saw you beating Jeanne Clinton. I think after it was over, he even went in and tried to help her, but it was too late. I think you let him out of jail to kill him, and you would have if I hadn't come along so soon."

"You must think I'm a pretty mean fella, Sheriff," Johnny said. "Next you'll even tell me you have a motive for me."

Both men were silent as the air conditioner's hum filled the room. Then Rhodes spoke. "I've got one," he said. "You were always a little hot tempered, a little fast with your fists. I think that with Jeanne you lost your temper when you tried to go a little farther than she wanted to go. You saw all those visitors, decided to have a little fun yourself, and didn't believe it when she told you that all she did for those men was talk to them."

"It's pretty hard to believe, you'll have to admit," Johnny said.

"I admit it. I didn't exactly believe it at first, myself. But it was true. Too many people told me for it not to be true."

"So Billy Joe was scared of me," Johnny said, changing the subject again. "Then why did he come out when I opened his cell? Why'd he follow me out? Why not just stay where he was safe?"

"I haven't figured that one out yet," Rhodes said. "It's bothered me some, but I'll get it if I keep after it."

"Billy Joe won't cut too much of a figure on the witness stand," Johnny said. "He isn't too smart, you know."

Rhodes let go of the chair back and flexed his fingers. He'd been squeezing too hard. "No, he surely won't. But with everything else, maybe we won't need him. It's too bad we don't have Bill Tomkins and Mrs. Barrett with us anymore."

"What have they got to do with this?"

Once again, Johnny's surprise looked real. He should have been an actor, Rhodes thought, not a deputy sheriff.

"They probably saw you, too," Rhodes said. "That's why you had to kill them. I really wish you'd stopped with Jeanne."

"Sheriff, I never killed anybody," Johnny said with sincerity and conviction. There was no quaver in his voice as far as Rhodes could tell. "I hope you believe that. I may have done some wrong things in my time, but I never killed anybody. And that's the truth."

"I'd like to believe that, Johnny, I really would. And if it is the truth, you'll be as much in my good graces as you ever were. We have to find out, though, and the best way to do that is for you to come on down to the jail with me. I imagine you can hire Billy Don Painter; you won't have to spend long in jail with him on your side. He'll get you a low bail setting, and you'll be out right up till the trial."

"There won't be any bail, Sheriff, or any trial," Johnny said. "I won't be going in with you."

"Yes, you will," Rhodes said. "One way or another, you will."

"If you believed me, I think I would," Johnny said. "But I don't think you believe me, even though I'm telling you the truth that God loves. And if you don't believe me, then I might have more trouble than I need if the case comes to trial." He took his hand from under the shirt in his lap. He was holding his .38 Police Special.

Rhodes stood there looking at the pistol. He couldn't think of anything to say, so he kept quiet. He felt a little like a fool. He would have felt more like one if he'd said something like, "You'll never get away with it."

"I'm sorry about this, Sheriff, I really am," Johnny said. "Now if you'd just take your thumb and first finger and pull your own pistol out of the holster, I'd appreciate it."

Rhodes did as he was told. The pistol dangled from his hand.

"Now lay it on the floor," Johnny said.

Rhodes laid the pistol down, then straightened. "If you're really innocent, Johnny, this is going to look mighty bad for you," he said.

"I know that. Ever since you came in, I've been trying to think what to do. Every idea I've had has been worse than the one before it, though, and like I said—if you don't believe me, a jury sure wouldn't. So I guess I'll just have to disappear."

"It can't be done, Johnny. This is 1986, not 1934. Bonnie and Clyde could do it, for a while, but they couldn't do it forever. I don't think you'll last as long as they did."

"We'll see. You'd be surprised at how easy it is to get lost these days if you know what you're doing. How many thousands of people do you think are living right on the streets of a city like Houston, pushing their belongings around with them in shopping carts? You think anybody ever stops one of them to check an ID? Hell no. Nobody cares. So don't worry about me."

"You wouldn't like living like that," Rhodes said.

"Maybe not, but it'd beat the hell out of living in one of those prison farms like we send people to. I wouldn't look good in a white uniform, and I wouldn't feel good crawling around weeding a field on my hands and knees. Besides, I never said I was going to Houston. I just said that's *one* way to disappear." He stepped closer to Rhodes.

"Now, Sheriff, I hate to hurt you, but if you'll just turn around . . ."

Rhodes didn't turn. Instead, he made a lunge for Johnny, who had apparently been waiting for just such a move. Anyway, he wasn't surprised. He clubbed downward at Rhodes's head with the barrel of his pistol.

Rhodes flung up his arm and managed to take the force of the blow with that instead of his head, but the pistol connected nevertheless. Rhodes felt the side of his head hit the floor, and then Johnny was kicking him. Hard.

Rhodes groaned as the kicks thudded into his ribs and tried to twist away. He wasn't able to escape, however. He was too weak, and Johnny was too quick. He could hear Johnny's breath coming in short gasps that sounded almost like laughter. Maybe it was laughter. Johnny liked violence.

Finally Rhodes lay still. The pain from his rib cage weakened him. He raised his head. Johnny kicked him again.

The next thing he felt was Johnny's hand in his front pants pocket. He must have blacked out momentarily, because he had no idea how he had gotten turned over on his back.

Johnny's hand was gone, then, and Rhodes heard shoe heels on the linoleum floor. He opened his eyes slightly. At the door, Johnny was putting on his shirt. Rhodes closed his eyes.

The door slammed. Rhodes rolled over, pain shooting up and down his rib cage. He knew that several of his ribs must be cracked. He hoped that the damage was no more severe

141

than that. He'd be in big trouble if one of them had punctured a lung.

He heard a car start outside. The county car. Johnny would have a beefed-up engine, and he'd be able to tune in the radio. He'd taken the keys from Rhodes's pocket. The thought didn't make Rhodes feel any better.

He tried to sit up, pushing with his arms. It wasn't easy but he made it. He edged over to the recliner and pulled himself erect, looking hurriedly around the room. His pistol wasn't there. Well, he hadn't really thought it would be.

He heard the county car pulling out of Johnny's drive, and forced himself to stand still. It wouldn't do to go to the door too soon and get shot with his own pistol. When he heard the car ease down the street, he moved. Slowly. Holding one arm wrapped around his ribs, he made his way to the door.

Johnny's pickup was parked farther down the drive. It wasn't exactly the vehicle that anyone would choose for a chase, but Rhodes didn't have much choice. He hobbled down the drive.

One of the things that both criminals and lawmen know is how to hot-wire an automobile. Rhodes took out his pocket knife and had the pickup started in under five minutes. It was an old green Chevy six cylinder, with a top speed of maybe eighty when it was new. Rhodes didn't have much hope of doing any good, but he backed it down the drive. At least there was more than half a tank of gas.

There were plenty of roads into and out of Clearview; three of them led eventually to major highways. The third, the one closest to Johnny Sherman's house, took longer to get to a major thoroughfare and wound through some pretty wild country on the way. Rhodes figured that Johnny would choose that one. It offered plenty of opportunities to turn off onto little-traveled county roads, and there wasn't much likelihood that there would be any highway patrol cars cruising in that area. Rhodes headed in that direction, praying that he was right.

The little Chevy chugged right along. Johnny obviously kept it tuned up, but he had a pretty good head start and Rhodes wasn't sure that he could catch up even if he had picked the right road. He was quite surprised when he spotted the county car only a half mile ahead.

Rhodes pushed down on the accelerator, causing the pickup to give a forward jerk, but without attaining any great increase in his forward speed. He groaned as his back hit the seat cushion.

Johnny must have seen him about then. The cruiser's blue and red bar lights flashed on, and Rhodes could hear the siren screaming. The cruiser began to pull steadily ahead. But not before Rhodes was able to get a glimpse of someone else inside.

It suddenly dawned on him why he was able to catch up so quickly. Johnny had made a stop. A little insurance. Rhodes cursed himself for not having thought of it. After all, his own house was so close by. All Johnny would have had to do was to ask Kathy to go for a ride, to have a little talk.

Rhodes shoved the Chevy's accelerator right down to the worn rubber floormat. He didn't know what else to do. He might not have much of a chance, but he was going to make a race of it, at least for a while. He had to get Kathy back, had to get her before Johnny killed her, too.

16

THE ROAD ON which Rhodes and Sherman were traveling was what is called a "farm-to-market" road. That meant that while it was straight for short distances, it was never straight for very long. Such roads often followed old farm routes and wound through the country without much regard to the principle of the straight line. In a way this was an advantage for Rhodes, in that Johnny couldn't use his speed as he could have done on a highway, and the pickup, with its short turning radius, was fairly maneuverable. On the other hand, the pickup was not loaded. The rear end was very light and tended to drift on the curves. It would be easy to lose control.

The pickup had side vent windows which Rhodes would have liked to open to direct some air on his sweating body, but he didn't want to lower the wind resistance any more than he had to. He decided to sweat. He wondered if Johnny had on the air conditioner in the county car and figured that he probably did. It wouldn't cut down the power too much, certainly not enought to allow Rhodes to catch him. Rhodes was in fact already losing ground, but he was trying to stay in the chase.

The irony of the situation struck Rhodes, and he almost laughed. He had been in car chases before, but he had always been driving the powerful county cruiser. He tried to imagine a movie in which a policeman was being pursued by an old pickup truck, but he couldn't do it. He knew that in real life the situation was ridiculous. He would need a miracle to catch Johnny Sherman.

The miracle came sooner than he expected. He lost sight of the county car for a few seconds as it went around a curve. When he saw it again, the bar lights were off and the brake lights were on. Johnny was slowing down. Rhodes looked at the road ahead and saw why.

About a mile away, just over the crest of a hill on the Clearview side, sat a DPS car. The trooper was positioned so that he could be out of sight of anyone approaching the hill while he tracked them with his radar gun. Johnny Sherman had no desire to go speeding by a highway patrolman with his bar lights on and his siren going. In fact, he probably had no desire to pass him at all.

A highway patrol car on that road, on a Monday morning, was an occurrence so rare as to be invisible on a scale of probability. It might not happen again for a year or more, but Rhodes was certainly glad that it was happening now.

In front of him, Johnny Sherman's car took a sharp left turn onto an unpaved county road. The recent rain had helped a little, but the Plymouth still raised a rooster tail of white dust from the crushed gravel of the road's surface.

Rhodes turned after him, choking a little as the dust sifted in the windows of the pickup. He was very pleased with the turn of events. He had traveled these roads all his life. There wasn't a turn that Johnny Sherman could make that Rhodes couldn't anticipate. It was like Bre'r Rabbit in the briar patch. And if the other road had been filled with curves, this one was positively snakey. There was no way that either vehicle was going to get much above fifty miles an hour. Even better, in less than two miles the gravel surface gave way to just plain dirt and clay and sand. If the road had been traveled enough since the rain, and if the ground had gotten wet enough, there would be treacherous ruts and maybe even very slick surfaces, both of which would put the Plymouth at a distinct disadvantage. The pickup was made for rough conditions and would be much easier to handle.

When Johnny Sherman hit the clay surface, Rhodes was

less than a half mile behind. He could see the rear end of the county car slewing around, so he knew that the road was slick and tricky. He slowed his own speed a bit. Better to be careful than to make a mistake.

Neither man was driving much over forty now, and Rhodes had to keep a firm grip on the steering wheel to hold the car in the ruts. The bar ditches off to the side of the road had very little water in them, but the weeds were bent in the direction of its flow. Apparently it had rained quite hard in the vicinity, and the water had run off fast.

The road twisted and turned past terraced fields and pasture, with neither man able to gain much ground on the other. Twice Johnny turned off onto side roads, and Rhodes realized that Johnny knew the country pretty well himself. And then he realized where Johnny was headed.

There was one portion of the county that most residents referred to as Big Woods. Blacklin County was not a major population center, had no industry to speak of, and was unknown to tourists. A minor oil boom had livened things up around Clearview for a time, but it was very quiet now. There were parts of the county that remained much as they had been a hundred years before, or longer. Big Woods was one of those areas.

Big Woods covered only about six square miles, but it was a place that could be very dangerous. People avoided it, even the people who owned the land the woods covered. The trees grew thick and tall, and the underbrush was almost impenetrable. Three years earlier a child had wandered off from a family reunion being held on a nearby farm and had gotten into the trees. Rhodes had headed the search party. They had searched officially for nearly a week, and unofficially for days afterward. No one had ever seen the child again.

There were deer in Big Woods, but there were rumors of other things less pleasant. Hogs that wandered off farms sometimes found their way there and raised litters that returned to their wild state, and no one doubted that there were

146

wolves there. Nearby cattlemen lost large numbers of calves every year to them.

Johnny Sherman had been a member of the search party three years before, and Rhodes thought he must have remembered the woods. A hundred yards inside, it was dark even at midday. Let a man get settled in the brush, and someone could walk within inches of him and never know that he was there. If Johnny got in there with two pistols, it was going to be very tricky getting him out.

They hit another stretch of graveled road. Rhodes could see the trees in the distance. Johnny Sherman put his pedal to the floor and the county car jumped ahead. Rhodes did the same, but with less than spectacular results. The pickup rocked and bounced along, sending jolts of pain zinging from one side of Rhodes's chest to the other, but he could make up little ground on the car he was chasing.

The weeds in the fence rows grew high here, and Rhodes lost sight of Johnny every time there was the slightest curve in the road. He knew that Johnny would get to the trees before he could be stopped.

Rounding a last turn, Rhodes saw the Plymouth stopped dead in the middle of the road. He threw on his brakes and managed to avoid hitting it by inches. Johnny was already out of the car and across the barbed-wire fence, prodding Kathy along in front of him with the pistol barrel.

Rhodes got out of the pickup and moved as fast as he could to the car. Just as he'd expected, the radio was smashed. There was no way to call for help, and there was no need to look for weapons. Johnny would have taken care of that, too.

Then Johnny called out. "Just stay right there, Sheriff. As soon as I get to the woods, I'll let Kathy go. Don't try to come after me before I get there. I don't want to hurt her."

Rhodes didn't believe him, but he said nothing. He went back to the pickup and jerked the seat forward. There was a Zebco 33 spincast reel attached to a cheap rod under there, along with a few tools: pliers, a screwdriver, a wooden-handled hammer with only part of a handle. There was also a walking cane. Rhodes took the cane and headed for the fence. Johnny was more than halfway to the trees by then.

Rhodes bent painfully and separated the second and third strands of the fence wire, holding down the lower one with the cane. He got his body through the opening, but his pants leg hung on a barb. He pulled to free it, lost his balance, and fell. The pain that shot into his head almost shorted his circuits; he barely heard the ripping of his pants leg. He did hear his own involuntary yell.

With the aid of the cane he stood up, feeling like a very old man. Johnny had heard the yell and turned to face him. He was taking aim with the pistol, but not at Kathy. He was aiming at Rhodes. Kathy was on the ground beside him. Whether she'd slipped or been hit, Rhodes didn't know.

Johnny didn't fire the weapon, however. Kathy launched herself at his legs and knocked him off balance. He struck out with the pistol barrel and hit her in the head.

Rhodes tried to run, but he couldn't move very fast.

Johnny looked back at him. "I'm sorry, Sheriff," he called out. "I never meant to hurt anybody, least of all you or Kathy." He turned and trotted toward the trees, which soon swallowed him up.

Rhodes traveled as fast as he could to where Kathy lay. Her face was smeared with mud, but there was little blood. She looked up at her father.

"Are you all right?" Rhodes asked.

"I think so," Kathy said, putting a hand to a knot that was rising on her head. "I can't believe this. I knew Johnny was acting funny, but he says you think he killed Jeanne Clinton. Then he dragged me out here, and he hit me. . . . What's going on? I don't understand."

"I can't explain it all now," Rhodes said. "Can you stand up?"

Kathy didn't answer. Instead, she got her feet under her and stood. "My head hurts," she said.

Probably a slight concussion, Rhodes thought but didn't say. "I want you to try to walk back to the road," he told her. "You remember how to start a car without the keys?" He had showed her once, in case she ever lost her keys.

"I think so," she said vaguely.

"Try to start the pickup," he said. "Go back to town and see if you can find some help. Talk to Hack. He'll know what to do."

"I'll try," she said, and started unsteadily across the field.

Rhodes watched her go. He could wait for help, or he could go in after Johnny. Either way was a loser. If he waited for help from town, Johnny could hide himself so well that no searchers could ever hope to find him. If Rhodes went in, he might not only lose Johnny, but he might get so lost himself that it would take him days to get out. *If* he got out. In those woods, it would be hard to tell who was the hunter and who was the game.

"Damn ribs," Rhodes said aloud to no one. He started for the trees.

Thirty yards into the woods might as well have been a hundred miles. There was nothing to see in any direction except trees, front, sides, and back. It was dim and still and hot; no breeze could penetrate in there. The light was filtered through hundreds of branches, and the trees closed around Rhodes like the waters of the sea.

Rhodes was not an experienced tracker, but Johnny Sherman was not an experienced fugitive, either. Rhodes could follow the crushed vines and the broken limbs fairly easily at first. But he couldn't move very rapidly. His ribs hurt, and his leg was scratched from the barbed wire. His pants leg flapped where it had been ripped. The footing was soft and uncertain, the ground covering as likely to give way underfoot as not. Rhodes didn't want to fall again.

A few hundred yards into the woods, Rhodes paused to listen. If Johnny was blundering along, Rhodes could hear nothing to indicate the fact. He heard a few birds twitter, and there was a woodpecker hammering somewhere not too far off, but that was all. He kept going, trying to keep in a straight line, laying about him with the cane to break more branches and limbs to mark the path clearly.

Another reason Rhodes went slowly was the possibility of a trap. If Johnny were to jump him, Rhodes knew he was a goner. He hoped it wouldn't happen, and he put the thought out of his mind. His shirt was sticking to his back, and sweat was running into his eyes.

Then Rhodes came to a deadfall. What had once been one of the larger elm trees in the woods had long ago fallen prey to blight, or lightning, or insects. In falling, it had brought down a few smaller trees. Now, brush and vines grew around the decaying trunks and almost obscured the rot beneath. Dead limbs stuck out of the greenness here and there.

Somewhere a squirrel chattered. There was no other sound. The area around the deadfall seemed unnaturally quiet. If Johnny were going to make a try for him, Rhodes thought, this would be a perfect spot.

"You in there, Johnny?" Rhodes said. His voice came out in a hoarse whisper. He cleared his throat as he waited for the answer, but there was none. Not that one had really been expected.

Rhodes looked the setup over carefully and then took a few steps forward. Johnny could be at either end, or he could be half a mile away. There were no signs to read. Johnny had become much more careful about things, which meant either that he was trying to throw Rhodes off, or that he was trying to trap him. Or that Rhodes had lost him entirely.

Rhodes took a firm grip on the cane and started around the end of the deadfall to his right, at the point where the huge elm had split and fallen. The cover there seemed to Rhodes a little less dense.

Just as he rounded the deadfall, he heard a noise. It was in front of him, not to the side, and he looked up. Thirty feet away, walking between two pecan trees, were several Poland China hogs. Or what had been Poland China hogs at one time. They were still black, and they still had the characteristic drooping ears of the tame breed, but they were clearly no longer the hefty meat hogs once bred on nearby farms.

These were feral pigs, the generations of breeding fallen away. They were thin and mean. Their backbones stuck up sharply. Razorbacks. Rhodes could see the tusks growing high on each side of their snouts. The largest of the animals had one tusk that was broken in two.

Rhodes heard them snuffle and grunt. They had not seen him yet, and he hoped that they never would. It was one thing to face another man with a gun. It was something else entirely to face feral pigs. He was about to turn and make a quiet retreat behind the deadfall when something struck him hard in the back. He suddenly found himself sliding forward on the ground, his mind wrapped in a red haze of pain.

He heard Johnny Sherman's voice. "You shouldn't have come, Sheriff."

"H-had to," Rhodes managed to get out. His hand felt for the cane. He heard Johnny walk toward him, and he wondered if he had just one more fast move left in him. Probably not.

Then Johnny noticed the hogs. Rhodes didn't want to lift his head, but he could hear them pawing the earth and rooting in the soil and grunting. It wasn't a pleasant sound.

"Godamighty," Johnny said.

While Johnny was momentarily distracted, Rhodes swung the cane at the deputy's shins, connecting solidly.

There was a sharp crack of cane against bone, and Johnny Sherman yelled out in pain. At the same time, he accidentally fired a round from the pistol he had been holding in his right hand. He stumbled toward the razorbacks, yelling and hopping from one foot to another.

The hogs were puzzled by his behavior and frightened by all the noise and confusion. A few of the more timid ones fled back into the trees, but two of the old boars looked up with a savage light in their tiny eyes. Their sharp hooves pawed at the soft ground.

Rhodes was trying to stand and having no luck at all. He got to his knees, however, in time to see Johnny turn toward him. Rhodes made a turning, clumsy twist toward his deputy, sticking out the cane's hooked end and managing to grab an ankle. He pulled, and Johnny tumbled down. He dropped the pistol, and both men reached for it.

Rhodes tasted dirt as his face was mashed into the forest floor. Sherman was on top of him, one hand on his head, the other reaching for the pistol.

Rhodes tried to raise himself and throw the deputy off, but he was hurting in places he didn't even know he had. Johnny squirmed over the top, getting his knee on Rhodes's neck. Rhodes managed to turn out from under him, but Johnny had the pistol again.

Johnny straightened and turned. That was when the hogs charged. Rhodes could barely see, his eyes being clogged with dirt and twigs, but he heard the sound as one of the hogs crashed into Johnny's back. All the air went out of the deputy in a loud sigh. The razorback didn't even slow down. It ran right up over Johnny's back, and its hooves churned the earth in front of Rhodes's face. Rhodes didn't move. He didn't even breathe.

Johnny was thrashing around. Rhodes could hear his heels striking ground. He could also hear the enraged grunts of the other boar as it dug its snout and tusks into Johnny's side. Johnny's voice came out in a continuous low moan.

Rhodes picked up his head and tried to look for the pistol. The other boar had returned, and the two were savaging Johnny as if he were a stuffed doll. His arms and legs swung wildly, but whether he was moving them or whether they were simply flopping, Rhodes could not tell. He saw the pistol and inched toward it.

He reached the gun and got his fingers around it. The hogs were grunting and slobbering; they showed no inclination to desert their prey.

There were four shots left in the pistol. That wasn't much against two wild hogs. Rhodes used the cane to push himself into a sitting position. He was hurting everywhere from the first beating and from the latest kick, and his hands were not exactly steady. He took a deep breath, held it, and then let it out slowly.

He took careful aim at the right eye of one of the hogs that was nearly facing him and pulled the trigger. The hog stiffened, and there was a high-pitched squeal. The hog took one or two stiff-legged steps and then keeled over, blood pumping from the eye socket.

The other boar looked up. It was the one with the broken tusk. It studied Rhodes as if wondering where in the hell he had come from. Then it charged.

Rhodes fired the pistol. The bullet struck the razorback's sharply ridged backbone with about as much effect as if it had hit a nearby tree. The hog didn't even slow down. The bullet appeared to have bothered it about as much as a mosquito. It lowered its head and came on.

Rhodes had not time for another shot. He twisted to the side to avoid the charge, yelling at the pain in his chest.

The boar didn't hit Rhodes head on, but it caught him a glancing blow on the hip. Rhodes yelled again, not even aware that he was doing it. He was tossed two feet to the side. He managed to sit up again and gripped the pistol with both hands.

The hog came to a stop, tearing up the dirt. For one horrible instant, Rhodes was reminded of a Bugs Bunny cartoon in which Bugs had been a bullfighter. The hog looked exactly like that bull, and Rhodes almost expected to see steam fly out of its ears. Rhodes would never laugh at that cartoon again.

The hog turned, lowered his head, and came back. Rhodes

had two shots left, but he didn't have time to think about it. He looked at the hog's right eye and pulled the trigger twice.

The hog struck Rhodes in the chest like a runaway steam engine. Rhodes dropped the pistol and went away from all the pain.

17

RHODES CAME OUT of it with a jerk. It was probably the pain that brought him to himself again. At first, he wasn't quite sure where he was or what was happening. He couldn't move his legs.

He lay still for a minute, eyes closed, trying to orient himself. Gradually the sounds of the Big Woods filtered through to his brain. He heard birds whistle and the scratching of insects. He heard Johnny Sherman moaning softly.

He pushed himself up on his elbows and looked down at his legs. The dead boar lay across his thighs. He struggled to a sitting position and shoved at the hog. It must have weighed three hundred pounds. It had a rank smell.

The shoving increased the pain, but he managed to move the hog off his legs. Then he had to lie back again.

He didn't know how long he lay there. He didn't know whether he passed out again or not. Nothing had changed when he opened his eyes again, except that Johnny was no longer moaning.

Rhodes rolled over and somehow got to his knees. He crawled over to where Johnny lay. The other dead razorback lay beside him.

Johnny was covered with blood, only a little of it belonging to the hog. They had ripped him up pretty badly, but he was still breathing. His breath was ragged and shallow, but it was there.

Rhodes twisted himself into a sitting position. Even that hurt him. He felt light-headed and dizzy. "Johnny," he said. His voice was husky and raw. "Johnny, you there?"

The deputy's eyelids flickered. "I'm . . . here," he said. It was barely a whisper. "Don't think I'll be . . . going anywhere real soon, you know?"

"I'll get you out of here, Johnny," Rhodes said, knowing that it was a lie. He'd be lucky to get himself out.

Johnny tried to laugh and wound up coughing. "I wouldn't try it if I were you, Sheriff. I think . . . my back's broken. Among other things." He coughed again and there was blood on his lips. "Wanted to tell you though. You . . . were right about some things. Wish . . . you could've believed me about it all. Didn't want to have to hit you. Thought . . . thought it might be easy to lose you in here. Should've known better, I guess." He stopped and breathed a deep, ragged breath.

"It all pointed to you, Johnny," Rhodes said. "I just wish I'd seen it sooner."

"Wasn't me," Johnny said.

"Too late for that," Rhodes said. "Too late."

Johnny was insistent. "Wasn't . . . *me!*"

Rhodes shook his head. Even that little movement hurt. "We went through all this, and it wasn't you? Give me a break, Johnny."

Johnny tried to laugh again, then broke it off. "I've got plenty . . . breaks I'd like to give you," he said. "Let me tell you something, though. I went by Jeanne's house . . . like you said. Saw the others there. Bill Tomkins, he . . . even drove his car. So one night I stopped."

"One night?" Rhodes said.

"Just . . . one. The night she died. Like you thought. I had in mind a little fun, like the old days. She was a wild one . . . then. But, no dice. Wasn't like that now. She . . . slapped me. I hit her back. She . . . spit on me. Batted her around pretty good then. Think I broke her arm."

"Yeah," Rhodes said. "Her arm was broken. Neck, too. You do that to her face?"

"Maybe the face. Hit her a good one. Not the neck, though. I . . . left the house then. She was hurt. Mad . . . as hell. Called me all kinds of names. But not . . . dead. Not dead."

"You did start the fight with Terry Wayne?" Rhodes asked.

"Yeah, I did that. Jeanne . . . cut me a little."

"You think a jury will believe you didn't kill her?"

"Sheriff, the way . . . I feel, there won't be a jury. I just wanted you to know. I hit her. I didn't . . . kill her."

Rhodes looked around for his cane and spotted it not too far off. He got over to it and pushed himself up. "I'll get you to a jury," he said. "I can get to the road and get to town. I'll send back for you."

Johnny laughed and then coughed. "Too . . . late. Time you get to town, too late."

"Don't tell me that, dammit. I'll get you out of here," Rhodes said.

Johnny didn't answer. Rhodes turned and started for the road.

He fell three times on the way out of the woods. The third time, he didn't get up for a while. Finally, he did. It took him a long time to reach the edge of the trees.

He could see the road when he got outside the woods. His vision was fuzzy, but he thought he could see three vehicles in the road. There was another pickup parked behind Johnny's.

He hobbled across the open pasture and saw his daughter lying in the weeds near the fence. He tried to run and fell again. This time he couldn't get up. In a few minutes, he felt someone lifting him by his armpits. "God dog, Sheriff," a man said. "You look like you've been in a tussle with a bear."

"Kathy," Rhodes said. "My daughter . . ."

"The girl's fine," the man told him. "I've got her in my truck. She's breathing and everything. Just a little tired, I guess."

"There's a man in there," Rhodes said, trying to point to the woods. Then everything went dark again.

The next time Rhodes woke up he was cold. He opened his eyes and saw a blob of orange, which gradually came into focus. It was Mrs. Wilkie's hair. Then it went away. He heard

Mrs. Wilkie's voice, however. "Nurse, nurse! Come quickly! The sheriff is awake!" Then Mrs. Wilkie was back, and there was a nurse in a white uniform with her.

"It's cold," Rhodes said.

"He's trying to say something," Mrs. Wilkie said. "His lips are moving!"

"I can tell," the nurse said.

"Cold," Rhodes said again. "It's cold in here."

"Can you understand him?" Mrs. Wilkie asked. She sounded frantic. Rhodes went to sleep again.

He woke up again. It was dark this time, or at least as dark as they ever let it get in the Clearview General Hospital. There was a light on somewhere around a corner, probably in the bathroom. He was still cold. He had time to wonder why they always kept it so cold in hospitals, and why they always covered you with only a thin sheet, and why the gowns they gave you were so damned skimpy—they didn't even have any backs in them.

There was a chair at the foot of the bed, and it looked as if there might be someone in it. He thought vaguely that it might be Mrs. Wilkie, though he hoped not. He drifted off.

The room was bright, and there was a doctor standing over him when his eyes opened. The doctor looked as if he might be eighteen years old. Rhodes had first realized that he was slipping over the line into middle age when all new doctors began looking about eighteen to him. He was used to it now. "Kathy?" he asked.

The doctor apparently had no difficulty in understanding him. "Your daughter? She's fine, nothing but a superficial cut and a slight concussion. She'll be in to see you in a little while, if you're up to it."

"I'm up to it," Rhodes said.

"You probably are. For a man who came in here looking

like he'd been run over by a Mack truck, you're in pretty good shape. The average man on the street wouldn't be too happy in your shoes, though."

"Shoes?"

"Not speaking literally, of course." The doctor ran his hands over Rhodes's ribs, which Rhodes realized for the first time were heavily taped. "That hurt?"

"No," Rhodes said.

"It will, later. Five ribs cracked, one of them pretty badly. But you'll live. Various other contusions, abrasions, and lacerations, too, but nothing serious."

"How long have I been here?" Rhodes asked.

"About thirty-six hours," the doctor said. "I'm Doctor Williams. I'm going on my rounds now, but just push the button if you need the nurse. Or I'm sure that one of your female admirers would be glad to get you anything you need." He turned briskly and left the room. The wide, heavy door sighed shut behind him.

Rhodes lay there, wondering about his female admirers.

He didn't have to wonder long. Kathy came in and stood looking at him. The hair was shaved back from her forehead, and there was a clean white bandage taped to her head. "I didn't realize that police work was so exciting," she said.

"Only sometimes," Rhodes said. "How do you make this bed work?"

Kathy helped him with the controls and got him into a sitting position. It wasn't exactly comfortable, but it wasn't as bad as he'd thought it might be.

"How's Johnny?" he asked after he got himself arranged.

Kathy looked at him, then away. She couldn't seem to find her voice. Finally, she just shook her head. Rhodes could see tears in her eyes.

"I was afraid of that," he said. "They have any trouble finding him?"

"I . . . I think so," she said. "It took them a while, and one man wandered off and got lost. Then they had to look for *him.*" She paused. "Johnny was dead when they got there. He'd been dead a long time."

"I expect there's been a lot of talk around town."

"That's one way to put it," Kathy said. "I guess if Mrs. Wilkie were to get naked and walk down Main Street, it might make as big a sensation."

Rhodes almost smiled. "What did Dr. Williams mean about my 'female admirers'?"

A trace of a smile crept across Kathy's face. "You do have quite a covey of fans," she said. "Ivy Daniels has been here four or five times, and so has Mrs. Wilkie. Ivy has been just fine, but Mrs. Wilkie has been driving everyone absolutely crazy. First, she thought you were going to die. That was bad enough. Then she caught on about why Ivy was here, and that was worse. Frankly, I don't know what they see in you."

"Me either," Rhodes said.

"People are really curious about what happened," Kathy said.

"You tell me."

"I really don't know. Johnny came by the house and said he had to drive out to see you in the country. He asked if I wanted to go. Things hadn't been too good between us lately, and I thought he just wanted to make up. Then you were behind us in his old pickup, and he started yelling about how you were out to railroad him for something he didn't do and how he wasn't going to take it. He was really mad. I'd never seen him like that. When he was forcing me across that field, he was practically foaming at the mouth. I think he really wanted to shoot you. And when I tried to stop him, he hit me." Her hand went to the bandage on her head.

"I'm not sure that he really wanted to shoot me," Rhodes said, "but I'm glad you stopped him just the same. His temper was his problem, all right. He admitted to me that he beat up Jeanne Clinton."

"You mean he killed her?" Kathy's look was incredulous.

"I thought so, yes."

160

"Oh," Kathy said. It was a small sound in the room, but she didn't add to it.

"I'm sorry, Kathy," Rhodes said. "I'm sorry he had to die like that."

"It's just . . . I don't know," Kathy said. "He was strange, and he certainly hurt me, but I just can't believe he'd kill Jeanne. Or anyone."

"He only said he beat her up. Maybe he didn't kill her. He certainly didn't have any reason to lie. Those hogs had worked him over. He knew he wasn't going to get out of there."

Kathy shuddered. "He wasn't the only one the hogs worked over."

"Yeah. Well, I had a gun."

"A thirty-eight! Nobody believes that yet! It's a wonder you're here at all! I'd think you'd have more sense than to go chasing a man into Big Woods with nothing more than a puny pistol!" Kathy looked ready to cry, so Rhodes decided not to tell her that he hadn't even had the pistol at first. Maybe later.

"I wonder how Ralph Claymore is taking this?" Rhodes said.

"Oh! Is all you can think about that election? When it comes out what a hero you are, you won't have to worry."

"I'm no hero," Rhodes said. "In fact, I may have been too quick to accuse Johnny. If I'd thought things through, he might be alive now. I imagine Claymore will love that."

"And you'll tell him?"

"Somebody has to tell what happened. Reports have to be filed. The paper will love it."

"Well, I think you're a hero. So do some others. Which one would you like to see first?"

"What about the jail?"

"Don't worry about that. Hack's called four or five times. He said to tell you that he's doing a great job and that he might run against you next time if you manage to beat Claymore."

"That old poop," Rhodes said, and laughed. He instantly

regretted doing so. "Good lord," he said. "Never make me laugh again."

"I'll try not to," Kathy said. "How about Mrs. Wilkie first?"

"You think Ivy would understand?"

"I'm sure she would."

"Then send in the redhead," Rhodes said. "If I can face that, I can face anything."

Mrs. Wilkie was not pleased. "I just do not understand, Sheriff, how a man such as you could risk his life on such a venture," she said. "I'm sure there was good reason, but . . ." She paused, waiting for Rhodes to explain himself.

"Line of duty, Mrs. Wilkie," he said, tight-lipped.

"Of course, of course. I understand. But this Daniels woman . . ."

Rhodes looked abashed. "She's a very nice person," he said.

"Very nice, naturally." Mrs. Wilkie shook her orange head. "But is she the right woman for an officer of the law? A man of importance in the county? I would think . . ."

Rhodes cut her off. "We're not engaged or anything, Mrs. Wilkie. I think she feels sorry for me. You know, a lone man raising up his daughter with no one to help him. I'm sure that's all it is."

"H-a-r-u-m-p-h!" was Mrs. Wilkie's only comment. She turned and walked stiffly from the room. Rhodes figured he'd lost another vote.

He didn't feel so bad about it when Ivy came in, however. She walked over to the bed and kissed his cheek. "I wasn't aware that you knew Mrs. Wilkie so well," she said.

"I believe she had the same sentiments about you," Rhodes said. "Let's just say that she may have been trying at one time to rumor herself into some kind of relationship with me. It didn't work, but I think she may have believed it would— eventually."

"Maybe I should try the same thing," Ivy said.

"You wouldn't need that kind of tactic," Rhodes said. "It would be a lot easier for you. Was that you in the chair last night?"

"Yes," Ivy said. "I thought . . ." She didn't finish her statement, but Rhodes got the idea.

"I'm glad it was," he said. "I'd much rather it have been you than Mrs. Wilkie, for lots of reasons. Sit down again, and I'll give you a few hundred of them."

She walked over and sat in the chair, while Rhodes started telling her what he had to say.

When Ivy Daniels left Rhodes's hospital room an hour later, Rhodes was pretty sure that there was a kind of understanding between them. Neither one had mentioned marriage, or anything about a permanent kind of relationship, but they both recognized the attraction and each knew that the other felt that what was between them would soon develop into something serious—and probably lasting. They knew that they would have time for talking later, and they suspected that they would be talking to one another for quite some time to come.

Rhodes leaned back against the hospital bed and rested. His ribs hurt now, and he wondered if he had, unaware of it, been given some sort of painkiller that was now wearing off. He thought about Ivy for a minute, and then he thought about what he would have to do in the light of what Johnny had told him. He didn't doubt that Johnny had been telling the truth, which meant that he would have to rearrange the puzzle in his head one more time. Pieces that had seemed to fit in one position would have to be placed somewhere else, and he would have to be careful not to force them in where they didn't belong.

It was too bad that Johnny was so hotheaded, that he let his emotions rule his logical side. If he'd only trusted Rhodes to see that he got a fair trial, he might be alive now. But Rhodes had thought him guilty. Would that have affected his treatment of his prisoner? If he was honest with himself, Rhodes had to admit that he wasn't sure. Convinced that he had the right man, how hard would he have worked to develop evidence in his favor? Maybe not hard enough. In a way, it was hard to blame Johnny for running.

Now the puzzle that had come together for him when Larry Bell had mentioned knowing Jeanne Clinton in high school would have to be scrapped. Well, it had been close, but close didn't count in this game. It could get you killed, but it didn't count. He'd have Johnny on his mind for a long, long time.

Unless Johnny had been lying. It was a possibility, even if it wasn't very likely. Rhodes reached for the phone on the nightstand beside his bed and dialed the number of the jail.

18

HACK ANSWERED, as always. Things were going along just
fine, he told Rhodes, except for one little problem. "You
remember them hippies?" Hack asked.

Rhodes remembered them.

"Well, we got us one. Hair down to his tailbone. Braided
kinda nice, though, like Willie Nelson wears his. Beard, too."

"You mean . . . Rhodes started to ask.

"No, I don't mean the beard's braided. I just mean he has
one. Could braid it, I guess. It's pretty long. Uses a piece of
rope instead of a belt. Don't even own a shirt, I guess."

Hack paused. Rhodes knew he'd come to the point any
minute now and didn't try to hurry him.

"Seems like he was lettin' cattle out of the pastures all up
and down Highway 11. Some of 'em went in other pastures,
but a lot of 'em just wandered up and down the road. Some of
'em wandered up and down the middle of the road."

"Any wrecks?" Rhodes asked.

"Two," Hack said, "but not bad ones. Killed the cows, of
course."

"Of course," Rhodes agreed. In any contest between a cow
and an automobile, the cow almost always lost, though the
cars were often demolished. Sometimes the passengers died,
but apparently not in these cases. "So what's the problem?"

"You ever try to round up three or four hundred cows and
get 'em separated and back to their rightful owners?"

"Three or four hundred?" Rhodes didn't think he'd heard
right.

"Three or four hundred," Hack repeated. "I guess you

wouldn't be up to herdin' cows in your condition, would you?"

"Not hardly," Rhodes said. "He must have been busy."

"Said he didn't think cows would like bein' penned up. Thought he'd give 'em their freedom. He hit every gate he could find for a long way down the road."

"How does *he* like being penned up?" Rhodes asked.

"Not worth a damn," Hack said. "But he might as well get used to it. Criminal mischief, I'd call it. He may not see the light for a while."

"Billy Joe still there to keep him company?"

"Well, now that you mention it, no," Hack said. "County judge found out about him and made us let him go. Said we didn't have no charges on him and we'd be up the old creek if the ACLU ever found it out. What's the ACLU?"

"Don't worry about it," Rhodes said. "I doubt we'll be bothered by them. Listen, Hack, there's something you've got to do."

"Just say the word, I'll do it."

"Get over to Johnny's house and look around for a .30-.30. If there's one there, take it back to the jail and take the butt plate off, if it has one. Soon as you get it done, give me a call at the hospital."

"Won't take long, Sheriff," Hack said. "Gimme about an hour."

"I won't be going anywhere for a while," Rhodes said. "Just take your time."

Rhodes had hardly hung up the phone before it rang again. He said hello and then heard the deep voice of Ralph Claymore.

"I hear you got the fella that killed Jeanne," Claymore said. "Mighty fine work, I have to say, even if I'm running against you. And you can be sure that I won't bring up a thing about it being one of your own deputies that did it. When I said I'd run a clean campaign, I meant it. I want you to know that."

166

Rhodes held the phone silently. "Rhodes? You there, Rhodes?" Claymore asked.

"I'm here," Rhodes said, finally. "Who told you that I caught the man that killed Jeanne?"

"What do you mean, who told me?" Claymore said. "It's all over town. Everybody knows about it."

"Well, everybody just might be wrong," Rhodes said. "I never told anyone that. They just assumed it."

"What do you mean?" Claymore said. His voice sounded suddenly unsure.

"I mean what I said. Nothing's been proved yet."

"Listen, Rhodes," Claymore said, "I know what you've been doing. I know that deputy of yours has been sneaking around asking questions about me. You're not going to drag me into this! I won't stand for it."

Well, well, thought Rhodes. Buddy must have been really worried about losing his job to do some investigating on his own. He'd have to speak to him about that. "Calm down," he told Claymore. "If you don't have anything to hide, you won't be in any trouble."

"I know it looks bad, Rhodes," Claymore said, a pleading note finding its way into his voice now. "But you've got to believe me."

"I'll think about it," Rhodes said. Then he hung up and did.

Hack may have taken his time, but it was less than an hour when he called back. "I done what you told me, Sheriff," he said.

"Good," Rhodes said. "Now look where the butt plate was. Are there any initials carved on the stock there?"

"Not a thing," Hack said.

Rhodes sighed. "OK," he said. "Hang on to that rifle for a while. Put it somewhere safe in case we need it. I don't think we will, though."

"Something the matter, Sheriff?" Hack asked.

"No," Rhodes said. "It's just that things would have been

easier right now if there had been some initials carved on that gun butt. I guess you looked all over the house."

"Sure did. I guess I could've missed something, but I think if I did you'll have to do some damage to find it. I didn't take up any floors or anything like that. You want me to give the place a real goin' over?"

"No," Rhodes told him. "I don't think you'd find anything if you did. Thanks, Hack."

Rhodes hung up. He'd had a bad feeling ever since Johnny had talked to him in the woods, but it could all have been worked out had Hack been able to find the right gun in the house. Since he hadn't, Rhodes would have to put his mind to work again. He already had a pretty good idea of how the pieces would fit. It didn't make him happy.

They let Rhodes leave the hospital the next day, not that they felt very good about it. He didn't feel too good about it, himself. His ribs felt as if someone were hitting him in the side with a sledge hammer at every step.

In another way, though, it was a relief to get out of the hospital and back into some real weather. The cold air in there had been making him feel even worse than his ribs. Air-conditioning was all right in moderation, but there was no pleasure in too much of a good thing.

Besides, he'd hardly been able to sleep at all the previous night. Every time that he dozed off, someone came in to check his blood pressure or to give him a pill or to shine a light in his face to see if he was asleep. It was the light that exasperated him.

So he'd spoken to Dr. Williams, who had objected to his leaving at first but who had given in when Rhodes threatened to walk out with his gown on and not come back. Williams had cautioned him to take it easy—no strenuous exercise needed. R & R was the order of the day. That was all right for Williams to say. He didn't have an unsolved murder on his hands.

Kathy picked Rhodes up and drove him home. "I've put fresh sheets on your bed," she said. "You can just get right in bed and watch television. I checked the schedule, and *The Searchers* is on this afternoon. You can watch that and get a good rest."

"That'll be the day," Rhodes said, in a lame imitation of John Wayne. "I'm going to eat lunch, and then you're going to take me to see the DA. I need to find out if we can go ahead and charge a dead man with murder."

Kathy swerved the car to the right, almost running up over the curb and onto a lawn. "I thought you said that Johnny didn't . . ."

"I said he beat her up, and I think he beat her pretty badly. She could have died as a result, I guess. Anyway, you're the only one who knows what he said, except for me, and I could have been addled when we talked. I was doped up and might have said anything. Right now, I think Johnny will be charged. If I change my mind later, well, we can worry about that when it happens."

"You'll tell me why, I guess."

"Maybe," Rhodes said, but she couldn't get any more out of him.

The district attorney was a young man with a shock of wild reddish hair that he could never quite get combed down. It made him look even younger than he was, and he always wore navy blue blazers to compensate for it. Rhodes suspected that he'd read a book about "power colors." Anyway, it seemed to work. He had a good record for convictions.

Of course they could charge a dead man with murder, he told Rhodes, but since Johnny had confessed it might be easier just to take the whole thing off the books. Was Rhodes sure that the confession was freely given and that Johnny wasn't just trying to shield anyone else?

"I didn't exactly read him his rights, if that's what you mean," Rhodes said. "But you'd have to call it a deathbed admission."

"Perfectly acceptable," the DA said, shaking his red hair.

Rhodes shook his hand and left.

* * *

At the jail, Hack and Lawton were glad to see Rhodes back. "Not that things have been too tough for us, you understand," Lawton said.

"Not a bit," Hack said. "We may be old, but we're still able to do this piddlin' little job."

"Course we did have one bad one this morning," Lawton said.

Rhodes waited.

"Case of a parrot in a tree. Kids let it out of its cage, and it flew up in a pecan tree in the yard. Buddy went out there."

"Worse than a cat in a tree," Lawton said. "With a cat, you know it's not going anywhere, except maybe higher in the tree. Parrots can fly on off."

Rhodes admitted that parrots could probably do that. "So how did they get it down?" he asked, knowing that he shouldn't have.

"Well," Hack said, "Buddy didn't hardly know what to do, so he just stood there lookin' up at it for a minute, tryin' to come up with some idea of how to get it down. While he was lookin', one of the kids came up with a rock and chunked it."

Lawton shook his head sadly. "Killed that parrot dead as a hammer," he said.

"Got it out of the tree, though," Hack said. "You got to admit that."

"That kid is goin' to make some team a fine pitcher one of these days," Lawton said. "You mark my words."

Rhodes was just glad it wasn't Buddy who had thrown the rock. He went out and got in the car, which had been brought back to town. It was time for one more trip to Thurston.

While he drove, Rhodes thought about what he knew and what he now *thought* he knew, and he wondered just how much the election meant to him, really. He knew it meant a lot, in a way, but did it mean enough to make him do something he knew wasn't right?

170

It wouldn't be hard, and it wouldn't be exactly wrong, either. After all, Ralph Claymore should have come forward immediately when he heard about Jeanne Clinton's death. Instead, he'd kept quiet and hoped he wouldn't be found out. Just like any other man would have done, maybe, but no other man was a candidate for sheriff. Hod Barrett and Bill Tomkins had kept quiet as well, but they weren't running for anything, much less the highest law enforcement job in the county.

So he could go public, tell what he knew about Claymore, back it up with witnesses, and probably win the election hands down. And if he could prove that Claymore actually had something to do with Jeanne's death, that would just be the cherry on top of the whipped cream.

The trouble was that he wanted to win the election because he was the best man. And not just that. He wanted the voters to choose him because he was the best, not just because they had no other choice.

All in all, there was nothing he could do, he decided, except follow his thoughts and the few facts he had and see where they led him. If Johnny had been telling the truth, hard as that might be for folks around the county to believe, then someone else had killed Jeanne and Mrs. Barrett and Bill Tomkins. And if those last two had seen Claymore's car at Jeanne's house, it was certainly possible that a desperate man might want to get them out of the way before they told anyone. How possible? Rhodes thought he would know soon.

Rhodes got himself a Dr Pepper out of the Coke cooler in Hod Barrett's store. He wiped the cold water from the bottle with a tissue from the box that Barrett kept nearby for that purpose. While he drank it, he watched Barrett wait on a woman who had gathered up a small order of groceries. When she left, Barrett walked over.

"You get the man who killed my wife, Sheriff? Was it that deputy of yours?" Hod looked old and tired. Even his spiky red hair seemed limp and bedraggled.

171

"I'll get him," Rhodes said. "It wasn't Johnny."

"Word's around he's the one killed Jeanne Clinton," Barrett said.

"It is, huh?" Rhodes said. "It was Billy Joe that robbed your store, though. I just wanted to let you know. You going to press charges?"

Barrett shook his head in disgust. "I don't care about that anymore," he said. "It doesn't even matter."

"He might try it again," Rhodes said, "Or someone else might find out how easy this place is to get into. Then you'd probably lose a lot more than just beer and a few packages of cigarettes."

"I'll take care of it," Barrett said listlessly. He walked over to his counter to wait on a customer who had come in.

Rhodes put his empty bottle in a wooden case and went outside. He got in the county car and drove to Elmer Clinton's house. The chickens were still in the yard, and the car was still parked in its usual spot under the chinaberry tree. Elmer was different, though. He was sitting in a metal lawn chair under the tree instead of inside.

Rhodes got out of his car. "Haven't gone back to work, yet? They must have a liberal leave policy at the cable plant."

Elmer hardly looked up. "Quit," he said.

Rhodes walked over near him and leaned against the car. It was coated with dust and chicken droppings. Rhodes tried to avoid the latter. "You ever do any deer hunting, Elmer?"

Elmer still didn't look up. "Some," he said.

"I expect you have a .30-.30, then," Rhodes said.

"Yeah, I got one in the house somewhere." Elmer sat with his legs straight and his hands crossed loosely in his lap. He was so still that only his lips moved.

"Would you be surprised if I told you I thought you had Hod Barrett's rifle in there?" Rhodes asked.

Elmer just sat.

"Why, Elmer?" Rhodes asked. He thought he knew, but he wanted Elmer to tell him.

Elmer looked up for the first time. His eyes were red and slightly unfocused. He didn't seem to really be looking at Rhodes, or at anything, except possibly at something only he was able to see. "What you mean, Sheriff?" he finally said.

"I think you know, Elmer," Rhodes told him.

"No. No, I don't," Elmer said, dropping his head again.

Rhodes kicked at a chicken that was pecking near his foot. "I'll just have to tell you then," he said. "I was asking why you killed Bill Tomkins and Mrs. Barrett, and I think you know why. But maybe you don't. I think they talked too much, myself."

Elmer stiffened, but he said nothing.

Rhodes waited a minute, then went on. "Somebody had to stop them, I guess. They were saying things about Jeanne."

"A whore," Elmer said, so softly that Rhodes almost didn't hear. "Called her a whore, and she was a girl that wouldn't do wrong for anything. Maybe before she married me, but not since. Never once. She was like an angel on earth." He shook his head sadly. "Called her a whore."

"And Bill Tomkins?" Rhodes prodded.

Elmer said nothing.

"He told me things," Rhodes finally said. "Maybe he told some others the same things."

"Lies," Elmer said. "All lies. About how people all came to my house at night while I was at the plant, came here to see my wife. How could a man tell a lie like that?" Tears squeezed themselves out from behind Elmer's eyelids.

"I guess you know I'm going to have to take you to the jail," Rhodes said quietly.

"What?" Elmer looked up, directly at Rhodes, his eyes wide, the tears running down his cheeks. "Take me to jail? What for?" He seemed genuinely puzzled, as if Rhodes had asked him to factor a binomial equation.

"For killing those people, Elmer," Rhodes said. "You'll have to go to jail for that."

The tears continued to run down Elmer's face. "But they

needed killing," he said. "They were the ones tellin' the lies. They had to be punished for that. I couldn't let them go around sayin' those things about Jeanne. They were *lies.*"

"Mrs. Barrett was wrong about what Hod was doing over here," Rhodes said, "but that's no reason to kill her."

"He was never here!" Elmer yelled.

"Yes, . . . Rhodes began, but he never finished the sentence. Elmer Clinton catapulted out of the lawn chair and charged him.

Rhodes shifted to the side, pain coursing up and down his rib cage, but Elmer managed to grab him and wrestle him to the ground. Elmer was yelling incoherently, and Rhodes was yelling with pain.

It was probably the pain that saved Rhodes. He was never sure later exactly what happened, but it seemed as if he literally ripped Elmer's arms from around him, grabbed the other man's biceps, and stood up. Then he threw him back into the car as hard as he could. It seemed later as if such a feat would have been physically impossible, but it seemed to have happened that way.

All the air went out of Elmer, and he sagged forward. Rhodes stepped up and tapped him on the jaw. Elmer keeled over in the dirt. A couple of curious chickens came over to see what the matter was. They scratched in the dirt by Elmer's head as Rhodes tried to get his breath and to fight down the pain that screamed in his body.

After a few minutes, he could breathe almost normally again. He looked down at Elmer, who was beginning to show signs of recovery, and took out his pistol. He wasn't going to take any more chances. He'd used bad judgment in just about everything so far.

Elmer sat up and looked around. He looked at the chickens, and then he looked at the gun in Rhodes's hand. He nodded his head as if to shake himself completely awake.

"We'll walk over to the county car, now, Elmer," Rhodes

said. "You'll be getting into the back seat." He gestured with the pistol.

Elmer got shakily to his feet and preceded Rhodes to the Plymouth. Rhodes opened the back door and nudged Elmer with the pistol. Elmer got inside, and Rhodes slammed the door.

Going around to the driver's side, Rhodes opened his own door and looked at Elmer through the wire that separated the seats. "You could save me a lot of time if you'd just tell me where that .30-.30 is," Rhodes said.

"It's in my bedroom closet," Elmer said listlessly. "In the back, to the right."

Rhodes shut the door and went into the house. In a few minutes he was back, carrying a rifle. He got in the car and took Elmer Clinton to the jail.

"Well, Sheriff," Hack began after Elmer had been placed in a cell, "I guess that about wraps things up, except for that little suit against the county. I sure hate to think that Johnny would've done such a thing as to kill Jeanne Clinton. And look at all that's come of it. It's a real shame."

Rhodes had to agree. "I think I'll go on home now," he said. "It's been a rough day. Call me if you need me." He left the jail and got in the car. It had been a rough day, all right, but it wasn't over and he wasn't going home. There was one other thing he had to do first. He started the car and drove away.

19

IT WAS GETTING late in the afternoon, and long shadows crossed the road as Rhodes drove past the former dump site to Billy Joe Byron's shack. Billy Joe's yard was just as exotic by the light of the fading sun as it had been at night, and Rhodes was able to spot a few things he'd missed on his earlier visit, like a heap of old magazines that were gradually becoming fused together as the rain and sun worked on them and four or five checkerboards that seemed to be laid out in some sort of pattern near the headless horse.

Rhodes crossed the yard, ducked his head, and stepped up on the porch under the low-hanging roof. "You in there, Billy Joe?" he called.

There was no answer, but Rhodes could hear someone moving around inside. "Come on out," he said. "I'll sit on the porch and wait for you."

Rhodes turned his back and stepped down into the yard. He sat on the porch and looked out over Billy Joe's Sargasso Sea of junk. It wasn't long before Billy Joe joined him. "You glad to be home, Billy Joe?" Rhodes asked.

Billy Joe shook his head vigorously. He still didn't want to talk, but it was obvious that he was happy to be at home, even though the stay in the jail had provided him with a bath and some fairly decent meals.

Rhodes didn't blame him for keeping quiet. What had happened was enough to scare anyone, especially someone like Billy Joe. "I don't mind that you ran from me the other day," Rhodes said. "You were scared, weren't you?"

Billy Joe nodded. "S-s-scared!" he said.

"You know you'd better stay away from other folks' stores, don't you, Billy Joe?" Rhodes asked. "You could get in big trouble like that."

Billy Joe nodded in agreement.

"And you've got to stay away from windows," Rhodes said. "Dammit, that's just not right. I guess Jeanne Clinton was nice to you, though, wasn't she?"

"Talk to me, sometimes," Billy Joe said hesitantly.

"Yeah, she was nice like that. She talked to a lot of people, and you see where it got her, don't you?"

"She hurt . . . bad?" Billy Joe asked, full of concern.

"Pretty bad," Rhodes told him. "You see what happened?"

Billy Joe looked agitated. "Yes. Saw," he said.

"You saw somebody in a uniform like mine hit her?"

Billy Joe was getting excited. "Thought . . . thought it maybe you! Thought . . . you!"

"It wasn't me," Rhodes told him.

"Know . . . wasn't now. You treat me good. Let me keep . . . smokes."

"Did you try to help her?" Rhodes asked.

Billy Joe nodded, almost shyly this time. "She . . . yelling. She hurt."

"So you went in to help her. I guess she was pretty upset."

"She . . . yelling. Said . . . words. Hit me!" Billy Joe's hand went to his face in an automatic gesture. "Hit me! Fight me!"

"You were just trying to help," Rhodes assured him.

"Yes," Billy Joe said, very excited now. He bounced on the porch. "Try to help! Face all . . . all . . ."

"Bloody," Rhodes said. "I expect her face was all bloody."

"Yesyes," Billy Joe said, making one word of it. "Blood! She . . . yelling. Fighting! Hitting!"

"You still tried to help," Rhodes said. "You held her?"

"Held her," Billy Joe agreed. "She . . . fighting." He looked at Rhodes. "She be . . . all right?"

Rhodes had been certain that Billy Joe did not know what had really happened. He had gone in to help the woman who had been friendly to him, and that was how the blood got on his shirt. She had been wild, maybe blinded by the blood from the beating Johnny had administered. It was possible that she thought Billy Joe was Johnny coming back. She had fought, and Billy Joe, trying to help and not knowing his strength, had struggled with her and probably caused her death.

Rhodes looked at Billy Joe. "No," he said. "She won't be all right."

"I . . . sorry," Billy Joe said.

"Me too," Rhodes told him.

They sat on the porch of the dilapidated shack and watched the sunset. Rhodes was a sheriff, not a judge or a juryman, and he wondered if he had any right to do what he knew he was going to do. Send Billy Joe to trial? Have him wind up in an institution? No.

Who would profit from it? Jeanne was dead and so were the others. Johnny's reputation would suffer, but he had beaten Jeanne and he might have done the same to others. Billy Joe never would, Rhodes was sure of that.

If Billy Joe were put in some institution, he would be fed and bathed, but what did that matter if he were taken from what he had, little as that was? He wouldn't last long like that. He wouldn't last a year.

A light breeze sprang up, and Rhodes could hear frogs croaking somewhere nearby. It was beginning to get dark. He had been wrong from the beginning, he thought. He had been nearly sure that the Terry Wayne business had been a setup, but it hadn't. He'd been wrong about Johnny. He'd seen Elmer Clinton's overwhelming grief and his sudden soberness after the first spasms had passed, but he hadn't thought until too late that Elmer might have become unbalanced. And then he'd been certain that Johnny was the killer. That might have been the worst mistake of all, but it was too late now.

Too late for Jeanne, too late for Bill Tomkins, too late for Mrs. Barrett, too late for Elmer, too late for Johnny. But not too late for Billy Joe. Out of all of it, maybe one could be salvaged, though he'd never realize it.

178

So Rhodes would keep the secret. It might be wrong, but he thought it was right. He hoped it was right.

Rhodes slid off the porch and stood in front of Billy Joe. "I'll see you later, Billy Joe," he said. "You take care of yourself, hear?"

"I . . . take care," Billy Joe said.

Rhodes walked through the surreal yard to his car. He got in and drove away.

The next morning, Rhodes was sore. His ribs hurt as badly as they ever had, and he could hardly get out of bed. But he managed. He looked sadly at the latticework of tape wrapping his upper body. Somehow he managed to get dressed.

Kathy fixed him scrambled eggs for breakfast. She didn't mention Johnny Sherman, and Rhodes was sure she never would. Johnny was a subject that would never come up between them again, and Rhodes had said all he wanted to say about it. He ate his eggs without speaking.

As he finished, Kathy spoke. "You seem pretty moody today. Worried about the election?"

Rhodes shook his head. He suddenly realized then he really didn't care about the election. "Ralph Claymore would do a good job," he said. "Maybe better than me. Maybe it's time somebody else took over."

"You don't really believe that," Kathy said.

Rhodes wasn't sure whether he believed it or not, but he was sure that the matter was no longer important to him. Having made his decision about Billy Joe, he was no longer sure where he stood in regard to his job. It was something he had to think about.

Rhodes pushed his chair away from the table. "Sure I believe it," he said. "How would you like having an unemployed father?"

"I wouldn't mind," Kathy said, taking his plate and brushing the crumbs into the sink. "I guess I could support you if I got a big-city teaching job. I typed some letters of application yesterday. If I'm hired, I could send you a little money every month." She laughed. "On a teacher's salary, it would have to be a *very* little, even in Houston."

Rhodes grinned. "I'm glad you'll be getting back to the city," he said. "I'll miss you around here, though."

"Somehow I don't think you'll be too lonely," she said. "If you don't make time with Ivy Daniels, I'm sure Mrs. Wilkie would be glad to come in and keep you company."

"A terrible thought," Rhodes said. He stood up. "I guess I'd better get busy and give the taxpayers their money's worth while I'm still in office. I hope I can get through the day without these ribs killing me."

Getting in the car hurt, and getting out of the car hurt, but Rhodes did it. His first stop was at a small brick building a block from the courthouse. The building had once been an insurance office, but it now bore a neat white sign with black letters which stated that it was the office of Billy Don Painter, Attorney at Law.

Billy Don was his usual well-groomed self, cordial and smiling. "Good to see you, Sheriff," he said, extending his hand. "What can I do for you?"

Rhodes shook hands. "You can tell me how you're going to proceed with this Terry Wayne thing," he said.

"Well, that's direct and to the point," Billy Don said. "We've got a mighty good case, let me tell you."

"I know that," Rhodes said. "I also know you can create a lot of bad feelings in this county if you go to trial with it."

"Well, now, that may be so, but what are a few hard feelings in the cause of justice?"

"Maybe nothing," Rhodes said. "But what's justice in this case? Terry Wayne may have been roughed up a little, but the man who did it is dead. You can't punish him any more than that."

"Ah, yes, punishment," Billy Don said, as if he hadn't thought of it before. Probably he hadn't. "What my client had in mind was compensation for the physical and mental pain which he went through. Who knows? He may be crippled

180

physically and psychologically for life because of his encounter with the rogue minions of Blacklin County's law."

"We aren't in court yet, Billy Don," Rhodes said, and the lawyer almost blushed. The tips of his ears got red. "I expect that Terry Wayne is working at his job right now, and has been ever since he got out of the jailhouse. If he has, we can prove it. We can also show that he wasn't any lily of the valley himself, I imagine. It won't be easy for you."

"I suppose it would also be easier for you if we dropped the whole thing," Billy Don suggested mildly, "what with the election coming up and all that."

Rhodes shrugged. "Believe it or not," he said, "I really don't care too much about the election. If the voters want Ralph Claymore, they'll get a good man. I'm just trying to save both you and the county some time and trouble."

Billy Don thought it over. "Perhaps a modest out of court settlement is what you had in mind?"

"I was kind of thinking along those lines, yes," Rhodes said. "A small amount, but enough to let Terry Wayne know we were wrong."

"I'll talk to him," Billy Don said. "That's all I can do, Sheriff. The rest is up to him."

"That's all I wanted in the first place," Rhodes said. "Thank you, Mr. Painter."

The two men shook hands again, and Rhodes left the office.

Things were pretty much as usual at the jail. Elmer Clinton had given no trouble. The hippie was calm. "Spends most of his time sittin' on the floor with his legs crossed," Lawton said.

"No other problems?" Rhodes asked.

"Not to speak of," Hack said. He waited about ten seconds. "Well, maybe there *is* one little thing."

Here it comes, Rhodes thought. He wondered if he would miss this routine if he were not reelected, or if he would be glad not to have to hear it. Somehow he thought he'd miss it, but maybe he could adjust. "What little thing is that?" he asked.

"Lou Willie Jenkins called," Hack said. He waited expectantly.

"How is Lou Willie?" Rhodes said. Lou Willie was an old woman, well beyond eighty, who loved to call the sheriff's office when she had a problem.

"She's fine," Hack said. "She's fine *herself*. But there's this one little thing that's not so fine." He waited again.

Rhodes waited as well. The silence lengthened. It was Rhodes who finally broke. "All right," he said. "I give up. What's the problem?"

"There's a skunk under her house," Hack said solemnly.

"She sure about that?" Rhodes asked.

"Sure as you can be," Hack said. "It's hard to make a mistake about something like that."

"I guess it is," Rhodes said. "She wants somebody to come out there and get it out, I take it."

"Right as rain," Hack said. "She figures it might die under there if somebody don't get it out right quick. From the way she talked, it might even be dead already. If it ain't, it could be dangerous."

Rhodes looked at Lawton. "You want to get it?" he asked.

"I'm too old to go crawling around under houses," Lawton protested. "Besides, I'm the jailer."

Rhodes looked at Hack. "Don't go castin' your eye on me, now," Hack said. "I'm older than Lawton."

"My ribs are busted up," Rhodes said. "There's no way I can get under that house."

The other two men just looked at him. "You're the sheriff," Hack said.

When Rhodes walked in his front door two hours later, Kathy came to meet him; but she stopped about twenty feet short. "What on earth?" she said.

"Just what it smells like," Rhodes said. "I've heard that if you soak your clothes in tomato juice, you don't have to burn them."

"What about you?" Kathy said. "Go on back outside."

"You've got a point there," Rhodes said. He went back out, and Kathy followed him.

"You'll do anything for a vote," she said.

"I didn't do it for a vote," Rhodes told her. "I did it for Lou Willie Jenkins."

"I'll bet Ralph Claymore wouldn't have done it. Come on around to the back and strip off."

Rhodes followed her. "Somebody has to do it," he said. In a way, he thought, it's not so much different from the rest of the job. "My ribs are killing me."

"I guess you won't feel like talking to Ivy, then. She called and wanted to talk."

"I can talk," Rhodes said, slipping out of his shirt. "I doubt that she'll want to see me until I get rid of this smell, though."

"What smell?" Kathy looked at him and they both laughed. Rhodes knew then that it would be all right. The smell would go away. There was a future for him, maybe a future with Ivy, no matter how the election went.

"You're right," Rhodes said. "I can't smell a thing."

If you have enjoyed this book and would like to receive details of other Walker mystery titles, please write to:
Mystery Editor
Walker and Company
720 Fifth Avenue
New York, NY 10019